# Dusky Nightshade
## and the Little Heathens

Trudy Silverheels

ARCHER TRENT, PUBLISHER
2017

While this story was inspired by actual events, it is, nevertheless, fiction. A few of the characters are real; others are loosely based on actual individuals; and others yet are totally fictitious.

ISBN 978-0999002902

**Cover Photography** © Monkey Business

Trudy Lynn (Bootsy) Silverheels
née Linda Yazzie
June 13, 1986 - September 17, 2014

WARNING

This book deals extensively with themes that may be deemed too mature or too controversial for younger readers. Parental discretion is, therefore, advised.

For Nana Tijinney

# I

## DAWN AND DULCE

A white Volvo station wagon came to a gentle stop at the curb in front of a 1920s bungalow. From the back seat Dawn Ramsey emerged and slammed the car door behind her. Then dumping her heavy book bag on the ground, she began fishing down the front of her school jumper for the house key she wore on a chain around her neck.

As the vehicle started to move again, Starr Logan, in the front passenger seat, rolled down her window and shouted, "Call me tonight. Okay?"

Dawn nodded and waved good-bye, then picked up her burden and trudged across the lawn to the house and let herself in. A quick tour of all the rooms confirmed that no one else was yet home.

Now began the best part of Dawn's day, the only part not rigidly structured. Mom would get off work at 6:00, when the bookstore closed, collect Meghan at the daycare center, and be home no later than 6:30 to prepare supper. Dad would get in around 7:00, and the family would sit down together to eat. Until then, or at least until Mom got home, Dawn would be completely unsupervised. She could do pretty much anything it suited her to do. Of course, there were not all that many exciting possibilities. Still, Dawn relished the hours and minutes she had to herself every weekday afternoon.

In her bedroom she deposited her book bag beneath her desk. Her saddle oxfords she removed and placed neatly on her closet floor. In the laundry room she stripped off her uniform and stuffed it into the dirty-clothes hamper, then padded out to the kitchen, poured herself a glass of chocolate milk, and chug-a-lugged it. The tumbler she dutifully rinsed before placing it in the dishwasher.

Dawn needed more of a snack than just chocolate milk, but could not immediately decide what she wanted. After staring into the open refrigerator for several minutes, she made herself a ham-and-cheese sandwich, which she sliced diagonally to create two triangular halves. She had taken but one bite when she remembered that she had not yet checked the post.

Ordinarily she would not bother, but today was her birthday, and she could reasonably expect mail of her own. Wrapped gifts would be presented tonight with cake and ice cream, but cards she might open now, and cards usually contained cash or checks. Last year she had scored nearly a hundred dollars on her birthday.

Dawn ran to the front door clad only in socks and panties. Before stepping onto the porch, however, she peeked out to ascertain that no one was about to see her. Modesty was not in her nature, but she could all too easily imagine the scene that would ensue should Ms Nosy Friedlander next door or Ms Busybody Ballard across the street call the bookstore to report having seen Dawn out of doors less than fully clothed.

Back at the kitchen table, eating her sandwich, Dawn sorted the letters. Junk mail went directly into the trash bin. Bills and personal letters for Mom and Dad went into one huge pile. Meghan received only a single item today, an activities magazine from some religious organization. The rest of the mail seemed to be for Dawn: six birthday cards with money inside and two small packages, which, when opened, yielded gift-wrapped presents to be saved for tonight's festivities after supper.

Dawn was counting her birthday money when the doorbell rang. She was not supposed to open for anyone she did not know, but from the living room window it was easy to see who was on the porch. And who was on the porch at the moment was the red-haired delivery girl from the German bakery downtown. No doubt, she had brought Dawn's birthday cake. Dawn opened the door without hesitation.

"The birthday girl in her birthday suit," the driver said with a friendly smile.

"It's not my birthday suit if I have on undies," Dawn pointed out as she accepted the white cake box from the girl. "Is *Robyn* really your name?"

"That's right. How'd you know?"

"It's on your shirt."

"Oh, yeah, I forgot about that. You're Dawn, right?"

Dawn nodded. "Yep. And by the way, I hope you won't mention to my mother that I answered the door dressed like this. She's funny about stuff like that."

"Don't worry about me. I'm the very soul of discretion. But I still have six more deliveries to make; so I'd better run."

Dawn placed the cake box in the center of the kitchen table, gathered up her loot, and went to her room to pick out something to wear. When the doorbell rang again, she quickly slipped into shorts and tee shirt, then dashed to the living room window. A UPS van was just driving away.

"Oh, boogers!" she exclaimed, frustrated at having missed a delivery.

She returned to her room and donned sneakers. What did she want to do for the remainder of the afternoon? Maybe she would walk downtown and window-shop. She might even spend a little of her newly acquired wealth. When she opened the front door, however, she found, lying on the porch, a large padded envelope. She had not missed the UPS delivery after all. Sitting on the glider, she opened the envelope simply by pulling a tab, and three books fell out, three books about tree houses and their construction.

Someone must be a mind-reader. For months now Dawn had been yearning for a real tree house. Her favorite retreat had long been a plywood platform high up in a pecan tree that had grown up adventitiously in the no-longer-used service alley behind her house. Dense foliage gave the platform total privacy in summer, if not in winter, but the platform itself was a bit shaky and large enough for only one person at a time. Dawn wished for something bigger and better, a private place she could share with her two best friends whenever they came over to visit, a proper tree house with walls and a roof, with windows and a door, and most of all, with a rope ladder they could pull up after them. So who was it that knew her so well?

Dawn glanced at the label on the envelope to see who had sent it and was horrified to realize that it was not, in fact, addressed to her at all. She had opened someone else's mail. It was easy to understand how the UPS driver had made the mistake. The street names were quite similar, and the house numbers were identical. Well, she would just have to deliver the parcel herself and apologize for having opened it.

The correct address was easy to find and not many blocks away. Dawn knocked, and the door was opened by someone she had known long ago, but had not seen in recent years.

"Hey! You're the story lady. I didn't know you lived here."

"I don't," the woman said. "I'm just visiting. You must be one of the children I used to read to on Saturday mornings."

"That's right. I'm Dawn Ramsey. We lived in San Antonio then."

"Oh, yes, I remember you. It's been a long time. Why, you're almost completely grown up. How old are you now?"

"Eleven. In fact, today's my birthday. That's why I thought this was going to be a present for me." Dawn held up the crudely resealed package. "It came to our house by mistake. I opened it before I noticed that it wasn't mine."

"So you're the birthday girl. Come on in. Leo wasn't expecting you quite so early."

The woman led Dawn through an enormous living room handsomely decorated in a manly style with dark green walls, hunting trophies, miniature bronze sculptures, Persian rugs, antique furniture, brocade drapes, a giant globe, model ships, several large landscape paintings, and more books in glass-fronted bookcases than Dawn had seen anywhere except in a proper library. Aladdin's cave could not have seemed more fantastic to her. From the living room, they passed into a dining room of more modest dimensions but no less outlandishly decorated. The chairs, eight in number, were actually upholstered with zebra hides.

"Are you coming?" Dawn's guide had opened the door to the kitchen only to realize that she was no longer being followed.

"Oh, yes." Dawn hurried to catch up. "You know, this place reminds me of a wizard's lair."

The story lady laughed. "Tell Leo that. I'm sure he'd love to hear it."

The kitchen was large, but quite ordinary and much less modern than the Ramseys' kitchen. Indeed, it seemed as if nothing here had been changed or updated since the house had been new nearly a century ago. There was no kitchen table, but only a butcher-block island in the center of the room.

6

One of two doors on the back wall opened into a tiny breakfast room with a glass-topped table for two. This breakfast room, bright white and sunshine yellow, was as lovely and as cozy as the kitchen was sparse and uninteresting.

"You can wait in here. I have to be going. I have a dinner date to get ready for, but on my way out I'll tell Leo you're here."

"Wait," Dawn said. "What's your name? I can't keep calling you *the story lady*, can I?"

"I'm sorry. I should have said. I'm Mercy Gruenewald. Call me *Mercy*. I live upstairs. Come visit me sometime. I'd love to see you again."

Dawn was confused. "Upstairs?"

"This house is a duplex. Leo is below; I'm above. My door is around the corner on the east side of the house. Be sure to ring the bell; I won't be able to hear you if you knock."

"Thanks. Maybe I'll stop by sometime."

Left alone, Dawn re-read the addressee's name on the package: *Leo Madrigal*. Well, at least she was at the right place. Mercy had mentioned the name *Leo*, had said, in fact, that he was expecting her. How odd! Had this all been an elaborate ruse to get her here for some sort of birthday surprise? Was it her mother's idea?

Five minutes passed, and Dawn was beginning to feel restless. In order to get a peek at the back yard, she drew the curtains aside, only to discover that the window looked out not on the great out of doors, but into what had once been a sleeping porch and was now a fully glassed-in art studio. On a huge easel, beside which stood a taboret littered with paint tubes, brushes, a palette, and any number of bottles and jars, an unfinished nude likeness of Mercy Gruenewald was easily recognizable. Dawn gasped.

Obviously, her mother was not in on whatever was going on here.

"Hello, you must be Dulce." The voice was a deep baritone; the accent, distinctly British and obviously very upper crust. "Have you been waiting for long?"

Startled, Dawn turned to face a surprisingly attractive elderly gentleman with such exotic features he must surely be of mixed race. He was standing in the doorway from his bedroom, and he was wearing only a bathrobe. His hair was wet. Mercy's hair had been wet as well, Dawn remembered.

"My name's *Dawn*, not *Dulce*."

"Oh, yes, of course it's *Dawn*. I do apologize. How could I have got that so wrong?"

"I brought this package to you." She pushed the padded envelope across the table toward him. "I was sure it was going to be a birthday present for me. I'm sorry, but I opened it before I even looked at the name on it."

Leo examined the address label on the padded envelope. "Am I to understand that this was delivered to your house by mistake?"

Dawn nodded.

"What an extraordinary coincidence! Thank you for bringing it. But now you must let me get dressed. Then we can begin. Do you want to wait here, or would you like to go on out to the studio?"

"How do I get there?"

"From the kitchen you can go out through the pantry. There's no way to get lost. And just make yourself at home. If you want something to drink, there are sodas in the refrigerator."

As Dawn passed through the kitchen, she helped herself to a root beer and then had to rummage through several drawers to find a bottle

8

opener. While doing so, she noticed on the counter top a beautiful handmade book with a leather binding. Making herself at home, as she had been invited to do, she carried the little book with her to the studio, intending to examine it more closely whilst waiting for Leo. But the moment she stepped out of the pantry, her full attention was captured by the finished canvasses that leaned against every wall. There must have been about two dozen, all of them female nudes. The painting on the easel was the only one of Mercy, but there were two of Robyn, the red-haired delivery girl, and three of a young woman Dawn recognized as a former soda jerk at the drugstore downtown. Indeed, all of Leo's other models seemed vaguely familiar. No doubt, Dawn had seen them around town; although of most she could not have said where exactly.

"Are you ready?" Leo had entered the studio by way of a door that communicated directly with his bedroom. He was dressed now in khaki slacks, a polo shirt, and huaraches.

"I guess so."

"Then why don't you make yourself comfortable in that big chair over there. I only want to do some preliminary sketches today."

Dawn sat where Leo had indicated. "Is it okay for me to talk?"

"Yes, but try not to move too much."

"I've never been a model before. I don't know how I should pose."

Leo was sitting on the divan to Dawn's left, drawing her in full profile. "Then it must come naturally to you, because you're doing fine."

"I've always wanted to meet a real artist. Are you famous?"

Leo laughed. "Only to my granddaughter and daughter."

"I guess you can tell I'm pretty nervous."

Leo denied it. "You seem perfectly relaxed. In fact, I've never had a better model. Your birthday portrait is going to be a masterpiece, I can already tell."

This seemed the perfect opportunity to clear up the mystery. "But whose idea was it? Why are you doing it?"

"It was your mother's idea, of course. And I'm doing it as a way of showing my appreciation for all the times she's sat for me."

Dawn was dumbfounded. It was beyond bizarre to imagine her mother's posing nude. "I guess you don't always ask ladies to take their clothes off, do you?"

"Not always." Leo was momentarily distracted as he moved from the sofa to a straight chair more or less in front of Dawn. "Why don't you alter your pose now? You could curl your legs up under you if you like. And don't worry. I'm not going to ask you to undress."

"That's good. I wouldn't actually mind, but I don't think my mother would be too happy about it."

Dawn continued to chatter mindlessly until at length she began to feel more at ease in her new occupation. Leo made a dozen or so large sketches with wax pastels on roughly textured earth-toned paper. After half an hour, he announced that he was satisfied and they need only set a date when she could be here at 9:00 in morning and stay until mid or late afternoon.

"Saturday's the only day I can come that early."

"Saturday's perfect. Would you like to see these sketches?"

10

Leo removed Mercy's unfinished portrait from the easel and propped his immense sketchbook there for Dawn to peruse. Then he excused himself to go into the kitchen to prepare tea.

Dawn found the sketches astonishingly revealing. In them she could see things about herself she was unable to see in any mirror. But were they true? She hoped so, for the girl in the pictures was vastly more interesting than she had ever imagined herself to be. When Leo called for her to come to tea, she picked up the little hand-made book she had found earlier in the kitchen, and carrying it with her, went in to join him in the breakfast room.

Tea apparently meant more to Leo than just tea. On the sideboard within easy reach of either place at the table was a large platter of cookies and cakes from the German bakery. The table was set with bone china, Irish linen, and sterling silver. Dawn was delighted. And when Leo held her chair for her to be seated, she felt her heart turn a little cartwheel in her chest. She had never before been treated as grandly.

"I see you've found my journal. Have you been reading it?"

Dawn blushed with shame, but shook her head in denial. "I only wanted to ask you about it. Did you make it?"

"I did."

"It's the neatest thing I've ever seen. Could you teach me how to make one like it?"

"You're interested in hand-made books?"

"I love books. I'm going to be a writer someday, and I've been thinking about starting my own publishing company too."

Leo poured the tea and encouraged Dawn to help herself to whatever she wanted. She would have liked to try several different goodies, but she knew that she still had to eat supper, then cake and ice cream. So she nibbled daintily at an oatmeal cookie as she sipped her tea. When the doorbell rang, Leo excused himself to go answer it. Left alone, Dawn opened his journal to the title page and read the three words written there in longhand:

*Observations and Contemplations*

She turned the page and read the following short entry:

*The beginning of Wisdom is thirst for Truth, but to grow in Wisdom requires Courage, Courage to pursue Truth wheresoever Reason points and then to embrace that Truth, however frightening it may seem.*

Thumbing through the book, Dawn read an entry here, an entry there. None was very long, a sentence or two at most. When she heard Leo returning, she quickly closed the book.

A girl of about Dawn's age preceded him into the room.

"It would appear," said Leo, "that we have two birthday girls today. Do you know each other?"

Dawn shook her head. "I've seen her before, but we've never met."

"Then let me introduce you. Dulce Flores, meet Dawn—uh—"

"—Ramsey," Dawn finished for him. Then standing and offering Dulce her hand, she said, "Pleased to meet you. He thought that I was you. I just figured it out."

"I remember you from first grade," Dulce told Dawn. "We weren't in the same room, but I used to see you on the playground and in the cafeteria."

Leo moved his own chair further around the table and held it for Dulce to be seated. This time Dawn did not wait for him to hold her chair. Leo laid another place setting for Dulce, and Dawn, hoping that she was not committing a terrible faux pas, poured tea for Dulce whilst Leo fetched an extra chair from another room.

"I guess you don't want me to come on Saturday after all," Dawn sighed as Leo was seating himself.

"On the contrary," he assured her, "I shall be very disappointed if you don't. Good models are always welcome here."

Dulce's plate, Dawn noticed, was heaped with cookies, one of each variety. Dulce would take a bite of one, then a bite of another, and then a bite of yet another. Soon every cookie on her plate was missing one small bite. When Dulce saw Dawn staring aghast at what she was doing, she explained, "I'm going to eat them all, but first I'm doing a taste test to determine which ones I like best. You know, for future reference. This is a chance I'll never have again."

Dawn just shrugged. What could she say to that?

Leo smiled tolerantly. "It seems a very scientific approach to me."

To Dawn, Dulce said, "People used to ask me if you were my sister. I guess we do sort of look alike."

Dawn recalled that she too had been asked that question. "It's because our complexions are so similar, I think, and also our eyes."

"I was hoping we'd be in the same room when we went to second grade, but you never came back after summer vacation. What happened?"

"My parents thought I should have a Christian education. I told them I didn't want to change schools, but they prayed about it and decided to send me to Berea Academy. I hate it."

Leo had heard of this Berea Academy. "Isn't that the school established by that radio evangelist? What's his name?"

"That's right," Dawn confirmed.    "*Darrell Wainwright*. Do you know him?"

"I know of him," Leo said.  "Two of my friends have had encounters with him."

"I'll bet they were unpleasant encounters," Dawn guessed.

"I take it you don't like him very much."

"You could say that."

The three of them chatted and lingered over their tea for another twenty minutes or so as Dulce continued to stuff herself with cookies.  Eventually, though, she was "too full to eat another bite."

"I hope you're not ill tonight," Leo told her. "Your mother will be so upset with me."

"Don't worry.  I'm not going to get sick.  I feel fine. And anyway, Mama's always cool.  She wouldn't get mad at you.  She'd just say it served me right for being a pig."

"Then let's go out to the studio and get started. The light is already waning.  Soon it'll be too dark to work."

As they all got to their feet, Dawn thanked Leo for his hospitality and promised to return on Saturday morning to sit for a painting.  She told Dulce that she was glad they had finally got to meet and expressed the hope that they might run into each other again. Then waving good-bye, she left by the studio's outside door.   In less than five minutes she was home.

By the time Mom arrived, Dawn had written thank-you notes to everyone who had sent her a birthday card.  She hated having such obligations hanging over her head; so she tended to get them out of the way at the earliest possible moment.

Homework was a different matter. Dawn was expected to do it as soon as she had had her after-school snack. But that was absolutely not going to happen. The hours after school were precious to her. She had no intention of sacrificing them to anything as uninspiring as schoolwork. Usually she completed her assignments on the ride to school the following morning. And since her grades in all subjects were consistently high, her parents had no reason to question her use of time.

Dawn's marks in deportment and spirituality, on the other hand, caused great concern to both her mother and her father, neither of whom could fathom why she was so defiant of authority and so hostile to religion.

Brent and Helen Ramsey had themselves, until four years ago, been nominal Christians at best. They had attended church only once or twice a year, used alcohol in moderation, and indulged regularly in worldly entertainments, such as movies and dancing. But then they had together undergone a conversion experience and become new creatures in Christ, whom they lived to serve. For their two daughters, they desperately wanted the same certainty of eternal salvation that they themselves now enjoyed.

But Dawn, to their great disappointment, would have none of it. She was utterly contemptuous of their faith. How, they wondered, had she developed such strong negative convictions at such an early age? And why did she so willfully refuse God's grace? It was a mystery that weighed heavily on them and threatened constantly to disrupt the tranquility of their household.

The celebration of Dawn's eleventh birthday was a low-key family affair. Dawn herself had steadfastly refused to allow her mother to plan a party for her entire class. Dawn had but two close friends, only one of which, Starr Logan, was in her class. Her other girlfriend, Peggy Wainwright, was six months younger and one grade behind. Last Friday Peggy and Starr had come home from school with Dawn, slept over with her, then spent the entire next day with her and slept over again on Saturday night. As far as Dawn was concerned, that had been her real birthday observation. Tonight was mostly about pleasing her parents. When the supper dishes had been cleared away, Dawn opened her presents. Then cake and ice cream were served. Afterward Dawn volunteered to help her mother with the dishes.

Later she shared a bubble bath with four-year-old Meghan, then got into new baby-doll pajamas and seersucker robe, birthday presents from a great aunt in Seattle. Dawn was anxious to telephone Starr, but wishing not to have her conversation overheard, she decided to wait until all activity in the hallway had ceased for the night. Finally, at around 8:30, she was able to make the call in complete privacy.

"Oh, wow!" exclaimed Starr, when she heard Dawn's news. "I can't believe how lucky you are. Nothing like that ever happens to me."

"Maybe I can take you over there sometime and introduce you."

"Do you think he might want to paint my picture too?"

"Sure. Why wouldn't he? He's always on the look-out for new models. He told me so."

The following day was Tuesday. Dawn wanted desperately to pay Leo another visit, but she was not expected there until Saturday. Would it not be presumptuous of her to call on him early? And what if he happened to be painting a naked lady? The last thing in the world she wanted was for him to consider her a nuisance. She would just have to wait four more days. It seemed almost too much to expect of herself. To occupy her time and to make certain that there were no chores for Mom to assign her on Saturday morning, Dawn spent the remainder of the week doing laundry and ironing. On Friday afternoon she dusted and vacuumed the entire house, put fresh sheets on all the beds, cleaned both bathrooms, and carried out the trash.

Helen Ramsey was astonished at this sudden burst of industry. "What is all this housecleaning in aid of, Dawn? Are you trying to butter me up for some particular reason?"

"No, I just didn't want there to be anything for me to have to do on Saturday except have fun."

"Have you planned something big?"

"Not really. I might want to meet Starr someplace. But I haven't asked her yet."

"How would you like to go to the caverns, instead?"

"I've been to the caverns. Remember? I went with my class. They weren't as interesting as I thought they'd be. And they're very muggy. I could barely breathe in there."

"Is there anything I could talk you into doing with Meghan and me?"

Dawn shook her head obstinately. "Mom, please, I just want to be on my own tomorrow."

"Okay, if that's what it takes to please you. But I think I'll take Meghan to the Children's Theatre. She's never been, and when you were her age, you used to love going there."

"If you're going to San Antonio anyway, you should take her to story hour at the library. That used to be my favorite thing to do on Saturday."

"What a good suggestion. Maybe I'll do that. You're sure you don't want to tag along?"

"I'm sure."

"You'll have to fix your own lunch."

"That's okay; I don't mind. Or I might just eat at the drugstore."

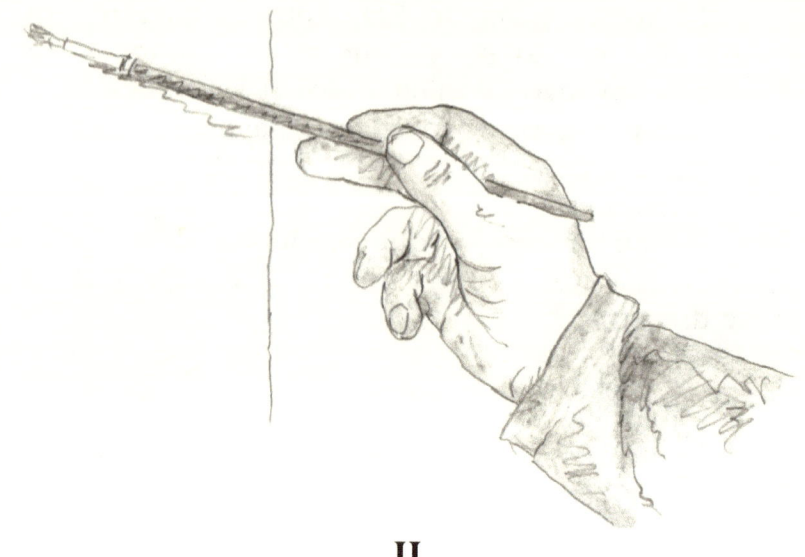

## II
## LEO MADRIGAL

On Saturday morning Dawn dressed in a short denim skirt, a western shirt, and cowboy boots. This was her favorite outfit and the one she wanted to be immortalized wearing. As soon as Mom and Meghan were away, Dawn slipped into her parents' bedroom to strike a pose in front of the full-length mirror there. "You look pretty damned cute," she told her reflected self.

By 9:00 she was in Leo's studio perched on a tall stool borrowed from the kitchen. Leo was standing behind his easel just eyeing her thoughtfully. Pretending to ignore them but watching, nonetheless, out of the corner of her eye, Leo's part-time housekeeper Petra was bustling about at the other end of the studio, dusting, moving furniture, sweeping, tidying up. Earlier, when Dawn had asked Leo if Petra were his wife, he had repeated the question to Petra in Spanish, evoking howls of laughter.

"Are you sure you're comfortable?" Leo asked. "Can you hold that pose for forty-five minutes?"

"I think so. Is that how long it takes?"

"We'll work for forty-five minutes at a time, taking fifteen-minute breaks every hour. We should be done by tea time. Some paintings take longer, and occasionally I have to ask a model to return for a second sitting, but only with much larger pictures than this one."

Petra was finished cleaning in the studio and was about to move on to the bedroom. In the doorway she paused to say something to Leo in Spanish. He laughed and made a reply that seemed to amuse Petra highly. She went away chuckling to herself. Leo picked up his brush, and with rapid strokes, began applying paint to canvas.

More relaxed now than she had been on Monday, Dawn sat silently and was amazed at how rapidly the first session passed. When Leo announced that it was break time, she was more than a little surprised by the difficulty she experienced climbing down from her stool. Her whole body ached. Her leg, neck, and back muscles had become stiff from holding the pose. She stretched this way and that and could not stop yawning. Finally, in desperation, she began a series of deep knee-bends. She felt like someone newly resurrected from the dead.

"How does hot cocoa sound this morning?" Leo asked.

"Heavenly, but first I have to visit the loo. That's what you say in England, isn't it?"

"That's right. There's one next to my bedroom and another across the hall from the dining room.

21

Petra might be cleaning in one or the other; so use whichever is vacant."

When Dawn joined Leo at the table in the breakfast room, she found him writing in his leather-bound journal. She sat down opposite him, took a tentative sip from the steaming mug at her place, then helped herself to a pineapple *empanada* from a platter on the sideboard. Shortly Leo finished writing and laid the book and pen aside.

"What were you writing?"

He pushed the little volume across the table. "Read it for yourself."

Dawn picked up the book, turned to the latest entry, and read:

Truth is not democratic.

She was not entirely certain what that meant. Other entries she had read on Monday were easy to understand, but this would require some serious cogitation. She closed the book and pushed it back across the table.

Leo raised his eyebrow. "I take it you don't agree."

"Not necessarily. I'll let you know after I've thought about it for a while. But what made you want to write it?"

Leo smiled sheepishly. "Whenever I'm working, only half my mind is engaged in the task at hand. The other half is remembering and analyzing arguments I've heard, books I've read, or questions that have been plaguing me for ages. Sometimes all that reflection pays off and I come up with new insights. When that happens, I write them down the first chance I get."

"Your little book is sort of like a bible for a new kind of religion, isn't it?"

"Oh, I don't know about that. I don't claim divine inspiration. The opinions are my own, not revelation, and anyone is entitled to disagree."

"Could I read the whole thing some time?"

"I'm afraid you might find it rather boring."

"No, I wouldn't. I like reading stuff like that."

"Then by all means, do. And afterward, I'd love to hear whatever you have to say about it."

"I'll come on Monday if that's okay," said Dawn. Then not wishing to seem overeager, she added, "Or maybe Tuesday."

Petra worked for Leo only half a day on Saturday. Before leaving at noon, she always cooked big pots of beans and rice or made *pupusas* or *chiles rellenos* for the following week. Leo was quite capable in the kitchen, but often he was too absorbed in his work to take the time to cook. Having food on hand that could be quickly and easily heated was more to him than a mere luxury; it was almost a necessity. Today Petra prepared a huge skillet of *fideo con pollo*. When she left at noon, Leo and Dawn had just completed their third forty-five minute session, and the painting was indeed beginning to look like it might be a masterpiece.

"I really like this picture," Dawn told Leo, "but you can't ever show it to my mother. She'd kill us both: me for sitting that way and you for painting me in such an unladylike pose."

"Oh, come now. I think you fail to give your mother enough credit. Surely, she's not so unreasonable as all that."

"Trust me. She is. I live with her. I know."

Over lunch in the dining room, Dawn resumed telling Leo about her mother. "She used to be completely different, but after we moved here, she started worrying all the time about sin and salvation

23

and stuff like that. Anything Reverend Wainwright says, she believes. I guess my dad does too, but mostly, I think, he just trusts my mom to decide for both of them."

"I take it you're not a believer yourself."

"I don't believe in Christianity, that's for sure, which is why I like your little book so much. It's smarter than the Bible and truer too. At least, what I've read so far is." Dawn paused only long enough to take a bite, chew it up, and swallow before continuing. "For instance, the Bible says, 'The beginning of wisdom is fear of God,' but on the very first page of your *Observations and Contemplations*, you said something completely different, which makes a lot more sense to me."

Leo was amazed at the depth of her perception. "So you're a fellow freethinker, are you?"

"My teacher calls me a *pagan*."

Leo laughed aloud. "I suppose that could amount to the same thing."

"My two best friends are pagans too. They go to my same school. And guess what. One of them is Reverend Wainwright's own daughter."

Work resumed after lunch and progressed rapidly. The painting was complete by 2:30. Dawn, concerned about having been away from home for so long, beat a hasty retreat the moment she was released from duty. When Helen and Meghan arrived from San Antonio at 3:00, they found her fast asleep on the living room sofa.

# III
## LEO'S JOURNAL

Dawn's homeroom teacher was absent from school Monday morning. In her place was a new substitute in the person of Jane Logan, Starr's mother. Immediately after roll call, Ms Logan asked Dawn to commence the school day by reading aloud from the Sacred Scriptures. This was a job that Dawn abhorred, and in the past she had simply refused to do it. But today, rather than disappoint Ms Logan, of whom she was genuinely fond, she reluctantly got to her feet and stood silently beside her desk.

"What's the hold up, Dawn?" Ms Logan asked.

"I don't have a Bible."

Ever helpful, Starr offered Dawn the use of hers.

"Thank you," Dawn said softly, then in a louder voice for the entire class to hear, "This morning I'd like to read from the King James Version, starting at Job 17:1. 'My breath is corrupt—'" Dawn paused, cupped one hand in front of her mouth and nose, crossed her eyes in apparent agony, then reached into her sweater pocket for a tiny atomizer, and sprayed a burst of Listerine into her mouth before sitting down again.

The class erupted into laughter.

Any other teacher would have sent Dawn to the office, but Jane Logan was secretly sympathetic to Dawn's rebellious streak. She considered herself a Christian, to be sure, but she was by no means a zealot. She had joined Reverend Wainwright's church twelve years ago at the insistence of her new husband, who had since died. Only in consideration of Starr's close friendship with Dawn, did she not now return to the far-more-liberal Episcopal Church of her upbringing and enroll Starr in either a public school or a secular private school. Today, an amused smile playing about her lips, she simply said, "May God bless to our understanding this reading of His Holy Word. Amen."

After school Dawn went directly to Leo's apartment without changing clothes or making herself a snack. She was famished, but so anxious to see her new friend that she could not bear to waste even five minutes. Hopefully, he would offer her something to eat.

"I like your uniform," Leo told her as he let her in.

"I hate it. It reminds me of my school."

"Nevertheless, you do look very fetching in it."

"Thank you. I should have changed, but I was in too big a hurry to get here."

"I'll bet you didn't get an after-school snack either."

"Not exactly," Dawn admitted.

"Then let's go out to the kitchen and see what we can stir up. What do you like?"

"Everything, but I shouldn't eat sweets when I'm already tired and hungry, because I always get grouchy afterward. I wish I didn't, but I do."

Leo suggested cold quiche and a spinach-and-bacon salad.

"That sounds delicious. Did Petra make it?"

"No, I made it. Would you like iced tea to drink? Or cream soda? Or maybe root beer?"

"Iced tea, I guess."

"Is there something else you'd prefer, something I didn't mention?"

"Oh, no, iced tea is perfect. I was just thinking about something completely different, something that doesn't have anything to do with food."

"Are you going to share it with me?" Leo asked.

"It's about those tree-house books you got from UPS."

"What about them?"

"I was wondering why you ordered them. Are you planning to build a tree house?"

Leo laughed. "I'll bet you think I'm too old for a tree house."

"Maybe. I don't know."

"I suppose I'd better tell you all my secrets."

"I told you mine," Dawn reminded him.

"You mean about being a pagan?"

"No, that's not exactly a secret. I was talking about my plans to be a writer some day and start my own publishing company. Nobody else in the whole world knows that; only you."

"Ah, but my secrets are so numerous they might require weeks to tell."

"I can come every day," Dawn offered hopefully.

"I shall look forward to that."

"Then tell me about the tree-house books first."

"Oh, yes, the tree-house books. The fact is, I have a granddaughter not much younger than you, and I was considering whether or not to build her a tree house."

"Where?"

"Probably right out there in the back garden. But if you think it's a bad idea, I'll just forget the whole thing."

"No, no," Dawn protested. "It's a terrific idea. I'd love to have a tree house myself, and if your granddaughter is close to my same age, then it's only logical to assume that she'd love to have one too."

"Still, it looks like a lot of work. I don't know if I could do it by myself."

"I'd help. I'm very handy with a hammer. And next Saturday my two best friends will be spending the day with me. I'm pretty sure they'd be glad to help too."

Leo considered carefully, scratching his chin. "I'd be foolish not to take you up on an offer like that, wouldn't I?"

"Very foolish," Dawn agreed.

"Alright, then, if I can count on you to help—"

"You can," Dawn promised. "You absolutely can. I'm totally dependable. I'd never let you down."

"Very well," said Leo. "When you've eaten, you can look through the books and pick out a design you like. Of course, I'll have to ask Mercy's permission. She owns this property. But I think she'll say yes. She has a niece who might enjoy a tree house on her visits here."

Leo set a place for Dawn in the breakfast room, then sat opposite her, drinking an O'Doul's whilst she ate.

"Tell me about your granddaughter," Dawn managed to say between bites. "What's her name? How old is she?"

"Her name is *Brenda, Brenda Louise Tolliver.* She's ten years old and in fourth form at St. Mary's Hall in San Antonio. That's where they live. Her mother, Carmen, is my only child. I see them about

28

once a week, but we talk on the phone almost daily. What else would you like to know?"

Dawn's mouth was too full for her to attempt to answer except by a little wave of her fork. *Please continue* the gesture seemed to say.

"Let's see," Leo mused. "Brenda visits here from time to time, usually for just a day or two, but next summer she's planning to spend several weeks with me whilst her parents are on safari in Africa. And to tell the truth, I was hoping you might let her pal around with you. She doesn't know any kids here."

Dawn's mouth was still full, but she nodded enthusiastically. She would adore befriending Leo's granddaughter.

When her appetite was appeased, Leo took her into the living room to select a tree-house plan. As she thumbed through the first of the three books, she asked, "Did you have to go to college to learn how to paint pictures?"

"No, drawing and painting seem to be second nature to me."

"I imagine you've always known you wanted to be an artist. Right?"

"I've always been interested in art, but it was never my profession until after I moved here. In England, I was a book conservator and not unhappy in my occupation. It would never have occurred to me to make a career change. I sketched for a hobby, but I never tried my hand at painting. Then Carmen's American husband was transferred back to the States. Naturally, he took his family with him, and that left me missing my daughter and my granddaughter almost unbearably. After only a few months, I closed my shop and followed them here. That was sixteen months ago."

"And that's when you started painting?"

"No, at first I hoped to resume working as a book conservator; but without the right contacts, I was able to drum up very little business. In fact, it was because I had so much time on my hands that I started painting just to dispel the boredom. Almost immediately I realized that a new career in art was what I really wanted."

"But it must have been wonderful to be a book conservator. I think that's a job I should truly love."

"I did love it, but I love painting more. Unfortunately, no one buys my pictures. On the other hand, I am beginning to pick up a few rebinding jobs, thanks to Mercy's recommending me to her many acquaintances."

"And the little book you made yourself, when did you start writing in it?"

"Not long after I took up painting. Writing and art seem to go together for me. Whenever I'm painting, I think of things I simply have to write down."

"The next time I come, I'm going to bring you something I wrote."

"Do you write a lot?"

"Pretty much." The next page Dawn turned revealed the most-beautiful tree house in the world. "Oh, oh, oh! This is it, Leo. This is the one."

"You're sure?"

"Totally and positively. This is the same exact tree house I've been dreaming about. It won't be too hard for us to build, will it?"

"I think we can handle it. Here, put a Post-It note on that page, and I'll draw up a materials list later."

With Leo's blessing, Dawn spent the remainder of the afternoon reading his *Observations and*

*Contemplations* whilst he typed at the desk in the studio. At 6:00, when she finally put the book down, she turned to Leo and said, "I have to tell you, this is great stuff. You really should get it published."

"I'm glad you like it, Dawn, but I seriously doubt that any publisher would see enough commercial potential in it."

"Leo, people need to read this; it's really deep. When I have my own publishing company, I'll definitely want to publish it. Will you let me?"

"Sure. Why not? Perhaps by then, I'll have finished writing it."

Dawn extended her hand to Leo. "Let's shake on it?"

Leo took her hand and shook it.

"That makes it official," she told him. "We have a deal. You won't forget, will you?"

Leo laughed. "How could I forget my first book contract?"

"And you're my first author. This is a pretty big occasion, wouldn't you say?"

"Indeed, I would," Leo agreed.

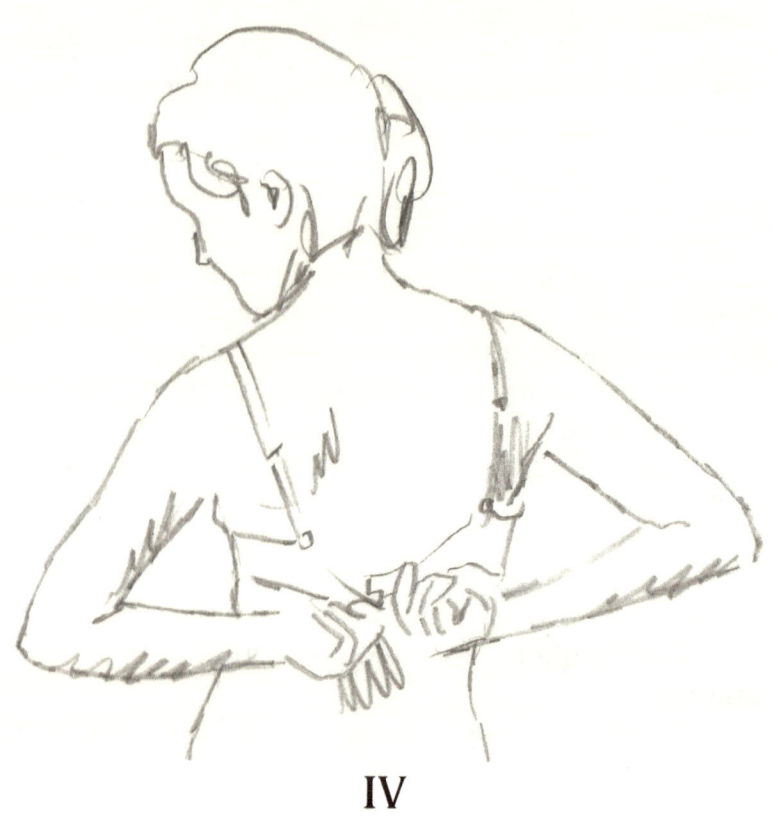

# IV
## MERCY

On Tuesday morning Mercy returned to the studio for her second sitting. But Leo was in no hurry to get started. He had just put on a pot of coffee and was about to make toast and poach some eggs. Mercy's own breakfast hours earlier had consisted of orange juice and cereal. She was easily persuaded to eat again.

"Where's Petra?" she asked, sitting down to table. "Isn't this her day to work?"

"You haven't heard? She's being deported. The immigration people picked her up over the weekend."

"Oh, that poor woman!  She's worked so hard to make a life here, and now she'll lose everything."

"I wonder what she'll be going back to."

"Where's she from?  Mexico?"

"I think so, but I'm not sure what part.  She once mentioned having visited Mexico City as a young girl.  And that's all I know about her past.  She came here about the same time I did.  She and her family have been living with three or four other families, also illegal, in a single-family dwelling.  I believe that's how they came to the attention of the authorities."

"What are you going to do for a housekeeper now?"

"I don't know.  Petra was one in a million.  Until I find someone else I like as well and trust as much, I'll just have to get along without any help."

After breakfast Mercy disrobed and assumed her pose from eight days ago.  Leo, of course, had to make a few minor adjustments, but soon he was satisfied that she was exactly as before.  He had only just begun to paint when the doorbell rang.

"Don't move," he told her.  "I'll be right back."

In less than three minutes he returned.  "Damien's here.  He's pouring himself a cup of coffee.  You don't mind if he joins us, do you?"

"Hell, yes, I mind!  If he wants to see me naked, he can be a gentleman about it and buy me dinner first."

Leo laughed appreciatively, but made no attempt to dissuade Damien from entering the studio. He merely picked up his brush and resumed work.

"Mercy, Mercy, Mercy!"  Damien exclaimed as he stepped out of the pantry.  "This must be my lucky day."

"You're a right bastard," Mercy said. "Did anybody ever tell you that?"

"I hear it all the time. I'm beginning to wonder if it could be true."

Peevishly Leo laid down his brush. "Try to keep still, will you?"

"Sorry," Mercy apologized as Leo re-adjusted her pose.

"My fault entirely," Damien said. "I distracted her. Maybe I ought to leave."

"No, no, it's alright," Leo insisted. "I overreacted. I don't know what's wrong with me today."

"Probably, you're just upset about losing Petra," Mercy suggested.

"Who's Petra?" Damien asked.

"His housekeeper. She's being deported."

Leo denied that Petra's predicament had anything to do with his testiness. "I'm terribly sorry for her difficulty, of course, but I haven't lost any sleep over it. No, I think that what's got me in such a foul mood is frustration at being unable to get my pictures into any gallery. I've sent slides to more than a hundred art dealers with no luck whatever, and yesterday a whole new batch of rejection letters came in the mail. Still, I do apologize for my shortness of patience. One never has the right to take his problems out on others. Can you ever forgive me?"

"Already done," said Mercy.

Damien changed the subject by begging permission to examine all the latest paintings. When he came upon Dawn's portrait, he held it up and asked the price. Leo named a figure, and Damien made a counter offer. Eventually a price was agreed upon, and Damien took the picture with him when he left.

Alone again with Mercy, Leo confided, "That was my first sale. I've given paintings away, and I've even bartered paintings for goods and services. But I've never before realized any cash money. It feels good. Celebrate with me tonight. Let's go out to dinner."

Mercy readily agreed. In the past she had invited Leo out any number of times. Nor had he ever demurred. But this was the first time he had asked her out. Of course, they would have to go in her car. He did not even own a vehicle.

Mercy's portrait was easily completed by 1:30, and as before (at the end of her first sitting) she and Leo found themselves in such an elevated state of sexual arousal that their falling into bed together seemed almost inevitable. Afterward, as she lay snuggled against him, she asked whether he made love with all his models.

"Oh, yes, of course."

"Really?"

"No, not really. I was exaggerating, trying to impress you."

"Silly man," she giggled and poked him in the ribs. "Tell me the truth."

"Why do you want to know?"

"It's not jealousy if that's what you're thinking. I'm not the least bit possessive or insecure. I'm just curious."

"Alright, if you insist, I'll tell you how it is. Since I've been painting, I've asked fifteen different women to pose nude for me. I've been sexually intimate with eleven of them. And every single time, it just seems to occur naturally. I've never once set out to seduce anyone, and when I ask someone to sit for me, my only thought is for the picture we shall create together. But if later on it becomes apparent that she is interested in sharing pleasure with me, then how can I resist? And why should I? The way it was with you is the way it often is. I don't begin to understand what's going on. I'm not a playboy or a manipulator, and I'm no Svengali. I'm just a struggling artist, who happens to get lucky more often than he has a right to."

"I know why. Want me to tell you?"

"Please do."

"I can only speak for myself, you understand, but quite probably, it's like this with the others as well. You're a nice man, Leo, and easy to like. From the very first, I've wanted us to be friends, even though I felt no particular attraction to you in a sexual or romantic way. Still, I was extremely flattered when you asked me to sit for you, especially considering my age. I'm forty-one, in case you didn't know. I've been around lots of other artists in my life, and not one of them has ever wanted me for a model. In any event, I was embarrassed to begin with, but you soon put me completely at ease, and little by little, I started enjoying myself. Maybe I've always been a closet exhibitionist. Who knows? What I do know is that hour after hour, I felt your eyes on me, on every part of me, and it was an intoxicatingly erotic experience. Then with my libido so over-stimulated, how could I not respond to an awareness of your desire for me?"

"You could tell how much I wanted you? Was it that obvious?"

"Leo, an inexperienced maiden could have read your desire. Oh, don't worry. You didn't leer offensively. That would have been a serious turn-off. But you communicated your feelings nonetheless."

When the doorbell rang, Leo glanced at his watch, then reached for his robe.

"Are you expecting company?" Mercy asked.

"It's probably Dawn. I'll let her in and sit her down to tea, then meet you in the shower."

"You really like her, don't you?"

"She reminds me of Carmen at that age, inquisitive and bursting with potential. But unlike Carmen, she's not getting the right encouragement at home. Anyway, she's a great model and irresistibly charming. I'd be very disappointed if she ever quit visiting me."

Five minutes later Leo joined Mercy in the shower, whilst Dawn, in the breakfast room, was happily eating finger sandwiches, sweet gherkins, and deviled eggs, all of which Leo had prepared in advance for her.

As artist and model slathered each other with soap suds, Mercy began telling Leo about having known Dawn in San Antonio years earlier. "She recognized me the day she brought your parcel. She couldn't remember my name, but she called me the *story lady*."

"So you two are old pals."

"Not exactly. I haven't seen her since she was four or five years old."

"What was she like then?" Leo asked.

"Quiet, shy, well-behaved, a good listener, and she almost never missed a Saturday. I could always count on her to be there right up front."

"What about her parents? What's their story?"

"I've never laid eyes on Dawn's father, but her mother was a regular library patron, and of course, she used to bring Dawn to story hour every week. I remember her as friendly, well-educated, well-bred, obviously affluent, very likable, an old-fashioned stay-at-home mom."

"These days she works full-time at the Christian bookstore downtown. I believe that's what Dawn told me."

"Then maybe I ought to stop in there and say hello."

"You hate places like that," Leo reminded her. "You've told me so a thousand times."

"I know, but I wouldn't mind spending a little money there in order to renew an old acquaintance."

"Dawn's parents are unaware that she calls on me. She's quite certain they wouldn't approve."

"I'll keep that in mind. I'm not about to give her game away."

Mercy was first to quit the shower and first to join Dawn in the breakfast room. When Leo finally showed up, he found the two of them engaged in earnest conversation.

Mercy handed him a tri-fold pamphlet. "Look at this, Leo. Dawn wrote it and published it herself."

Leo examined the pamphlet with interest. "A religious tract?"

"I guess you could call it that," Dawn admitted.

"It's not an apology," Mercy explained, "but a polemic. And very persuasive. You have to read it."

"It says, 'by Dusky Nightshade.' Is that your *nom de discrétion*?"

Dawn nodded. "The reason I have to use a secret pen name is because I can't let my parents know what I'm up to. This isn't the only tract I've done, but it is the best. If you like it, I'll let you read the others too."

Leo spent the next few minutes carefully reading and re-reading Dawn's paper. He was astonished not only at the sophistication of her arguments, but also at the competence of her composition. For once in his life, he simply did not know what to say.

"You don't like it, do you? Tell me what's wrong with it, and don't worry about hurting my feelings. I can't learn how to do better without criticism."

"Did you really write this yourself?"

Dawn nodded affirmatively.

"And the idea for it, where did that come from?"

"Out of my head, I guess. Nobody told me to write it. In fact, you and Mercy are the only ones who know about it."

Leo scratched his head. "Dawn, this is outstanding. I am in absolute awe of your genius. But I'd still like to understand how you came up with the idea to do this."

"I don't really know. I guess seeing all those religious tracts I disagreed with must have made me want to write an answer to them."

"Are you familiar with Percy Shelley?" Leo asked.

"Wasn't he the one that wrote *Frankenstein*?"

"No, his wife Mary wrote *Frankenstein*. Percy was a poet. But in his university days he wrote and published a pamphlet in support of atheism. I have a facsimile of that pamphlet. Would you care to see it?"

"Oh, yes, very much."

Leo excused himself and went to the living room to retrieve the item.

Dawn turned to Mercy and said, "You know, one of the people I admire most in history is Thomas Paine. Maybe that's another reason I decided to become a pamphleteer myself."

"Do you have a plan for distribution?"

Dawn confessed that she did not. "I've thought about it and thought about it, and the only thing I'm sure of is that I don't want to just hand my literature out on the street, the way those Pentecostal ladies do."

"No," Mercy agreed with her, "I don't think that's a very good idea. Maybe I can help you out. Let me talk to some people I know."

A moment later Leo returned with the Shelley pamphlet. Dawn immediately began reading it. Mercy got to her feet and bade Dawn and Leo good-bye and promised Leo that she would be ready at 7:00 to go out to dinner.

# V

## THE TREE HOUSE

Tree-house construction began on Wednesday. Leo called the lumber yard early, and a truck-load of building materials was delivered before noon. When Dawn arrived to help, she found the rough framing already done and the deck nearly complete.

"I see you've changed clothes today," said Leo, climbing down to meet her. "Did you also eat, or would you like a snack?"

"I didn't eat. I was hoping you'd offer me something."

"You're in luck then. You'll find a cheese plate in the refrigerator, and you can help yourself to whatever you'd like to drink. I'm going to keep working. I want to get a safety rail around the deck before you go up."

In Leo's refrigerator Dawn found the Saran-wrapped platter, which included a variety of cheeses and an assortment of nuts and dried fruits. On the breakfast table was a box of Triscuits with her name on it. To drink, she chose an O'Doul's, simply because she had never had one and because it seemed to be Leo's favorite cold beverage. She loved trying new things, but she did not at first care for the taste of O'Doul's. However, hating waste as she did, she refused to pour it out, and after a few more swallows, she decided that she quite liked it. When she had eaten all she wanted, she tidied up after herself, carefully resealed the plastic wrap on the cheese plate, and returned it to the refrigerator. Then she removed one more O'Doul's and took it out to Leo.

"Bless your heart!" he said, taking the can from her. "I was really needing that."

"It's not beer, is it? The can says it's non-alcoholic."

"It is beer, but without the alcohol. I hope you didn't drink one."

"I did. Am I going to get drunk?"

Leo laughed. "No, it won't make you drunk. It won't hurt you in any way whatever, but on your breath, it'll smell exactly like any beer. I wouldn't want your parents wondering who's been plying you with alcohol."

Dawn was seriously concerned. "What can I do?"

"It's a long time till 6:30. Maybe by then no one will notice."

Dawn took the little atomizer from her pocket and sprayed a burst of Listerine into her mouth. "This will help too, I hope. And I'll try not to get too close to anybody tonight. By tomorrow the beer smell should be completely gone, right?"

"I should imagine so," Leo concurred.

When he finished his O'Doul's, he tied a nail apron around Dawn's waist and presented her with a brand new light-weight hammer. Then as she knelt on the deck, attaching lap siding to the tree house, he laid shingles on the roof. By quitting time the tree house was very nearly ready for occupancy. It wanted only paint, and paint could wait until Saturday.

In the studio, Dawn reclined on the sofa. Leo sat in an overstuffed chair reading the new pamphlets she had brought today. Some dealt with religious matters, others with social issues, and others yet with pure philosophy.

"How did you learn to write so well?" Leo asked her.

"Oh, that's easy. I had a really good composition teacher. Mr Wynter could teach anybody how to be an author. Too bad he doesn't work there anymore! Reverend Wainwright didn't get along with him, because he wasn't religious enough, but he was the only good thing about that school."

Leo had heard the story before. "Damien Wynter is a good friend of mine. It was he, by the way, who bought your picture."

Dawn sat upright. "Mr Wynter bought the painting you did of me? I didn't even know you'd sold it."

"Yesterday."

"This is so amazing! You and Mr Wynter know each other. But why did he want my picture? He's probably going to throw darts at it. I used to be what you might call a 'disruptive influence' in his class."

"He didn't mention that. In fact, he didn't mention that he knew you. He's decorating his home, and he seemed to think that painting of you was just right for his living room."

Dawn smiled broadly. "I guess I turned out to be a pretty wonderful model for you, didn't I? You can paint me again sometime if you want to."

"Count on it."

On Thursday, when Leo came to the door, the first words out of Dawn's mouth were these: "I've been meaning to ask you. Did you ever paint that portrait of Dulce?"

"Yes, last Sunday. Her mother picked it up about an hour ago."

"Boogers! I wanted to see it."

"Sorry. It's been here all week. You could have seen it any time."

"Oh, well, I guess it doesn't matter. I was just curious."

In the studio, Dawn re-examined Leo's finished and unfinished paintings and asked the identity of the model for each. She was particularly interested to know which pictures were of Dulce's mother. When her curiosity was satisfied, hunger became her most-pressing issue.

Leo heated up some pizza left over from lunch and made Greek salad. Dawn set two places at the little breakfast table and opened a root beer for herself and an O'Doul's for him. Then they sat down opposite each other to eat.

"Leo," said Dawn, "can I ask you something? I mean, may I?"

"What's on your mind?"

"That pamphlet about atheism, it was kind of hard to understand. The sentences were all twisty."

"I am sure I must have read that pamphlet at some point, but I cannot now recall what Shelley's arguments were. It seems to me that a thinking person cannot but doubt the existence of God; and yet it is a trap to try to make a case for atheism. It is more sensible to claim only to be an agnostic. Are you familiar with that term?"

"I think so. It means you don't know what to believe. Right?"

"I like to say that I'm keeping an open mind until all the evidence is in. In fact, I do not even suspect that God may be real, but knowing that I cannot disprove His being, I don't feel that I have the right to say that I'm an atheist."

"That makes sense, I suppose, but as for me, I am an atheist. And it doesn't bother me one bit that

I can't prove that God isn't real. I can't prove that Santa Claus isn't real either, but I still know he's just a myth, the same as fairies and mermaids. Nobody can ever prove that anything does not exist. But on the other hand, it shouldn't be too hard to prove that something real does exist. So let the people who believe in God be the ones to come up with the proof."

"Well, aren't you a clever little heathen! That was the most eloquent argument I've ever heard in defense of atheism. I am completely persuaded. From this day forth, I shall proudly own up to being an atheist myself."

On Friday of that week, school let out early for a teachers' meeting; and so it happened that Dawn arrived at Leo's apartment only a little after mid-day to find him at work on a new painting. Leo invited her in, but warned her that she might have to leave should his model be too uncomfortable with her presence.

He need not have been concerned, however; Christi Broughton was totally relaxed in her natural state. Nor did the constant parade of visitors through the studio cause her the least embarrassment. Recently separated from her husband of two years, she was rooming with Mercy whilst searching for a job and an apartment of her own. Mercy had accompanied her to Leo's studio this morning and had remained with her for the first hour of her sitting. Then Damien had stopped by briefly, and later two applicants for the position of housekeeper. Leo had conducted both job interviews in the studio as he painted. Now this child had come to watch, and for the first time Leo was worried that Christi might object.

"I didn't mind about anybody else. Why should I mind about her?"

Dawn brought out the kitchen stool and perched upon it where she could see approximately what Leo was seeing of his model and observe how he applied paint to canvas. It was for her an intriguing process. But of the sexual tension between artist and model, Dawn remained unaware. When Leo announced break time, Christi slipped on a silk kimono; and the three of them had tea and muffins at the dining table. Then the sitting resumed. As the painting neared completion, Christi began hinting—subtly to begin with and then less subtly—that it was getting to be time for Dawn to go.

Because it was still too early to return home, Dawn decided to visit Mercy instead. She rang the bell and waited several minutes before Mercy opened up and let her in. To reach the apartment above they had to climb a long, straight flight of stairs to a small landing, and then pass through another security door. Mercy's apartment was laid out almost exactly as was Leo's, with the exception that there had never been a sleeping porch at the rear. Her kitchen pantry was a dead end, and her breakfast-room window looked directly out on the backyard (beyond the roof of the studio). The books in her living room were as numerous as Leo's. But her décor was more traditional. The colors employed here were chocolate, off white, and muted pastels, similar hues to those of the Ramsey home. Wall art consisted of photographs, water colors, etchings, serigraphs, and lithographs, none of those in the living room being in any way erotic. The pictures in the master bedroom, however, were all framed charcoal drawings of a male model.

"I did these myself," Mercy said when Dawn asked. "In my student days, I used to imagine that I might someday make a career of art, but it didn't work out. I had the talent, but not the temperament, and I lacked commitment."

"Weren't you embarrassed drawing a naked man?"

"Oh, yes, but I tried not to show it. I wanted everyone to believe that I was a sophisticated woman of the world. And of course, when I came home at the end of term, I felt deliciously wicked showing all my nude drawings to friends and family."

"What did your parents say? Were they upset?"

Mercy smiled, remembering. "My father's an Episcopal priest, you know, but a lot less stuffy than one might expect. His only comment was, 'Personally speaking, I'd rather see pictures of naked women, but I suppose these aren't half bad.' My mother, on the other hand, is very prudish, although not very out-spoken. She just sniffed and turned away. My grand-mother's the one that broke me up. She examined all the pictures very minutely, then said, 'These are very good, dear, but I can't help wondering if this man's penis is really so small.'"

Dawn laughed aloud and clapped her hands in glee. "What'd you say to that?"

"I said, 'It's much larger erect.'"

"What's that mean?" Dawn asked.

"Oh, my! I guess I forgot how young you are. I should never have told you that in the first place."

"No, please, it's okay. Just tell me what *erect* means. I thought it had something to do with construction. If it's about sex, I want to know. I won't repeat anything you say. I'm very good at keeping secrets."

"No, Dawn, I've said too much already. You can look it up in the dictionary sometime."

48

# VI

## STARR

The city of New Braunfels was originally built at the foot of the Balcones Escarpment, which for ensuing decades constituted the community's natural boundary on the west. This escarpment, understand, is not a sheer cliff, but only a perilously steep and densely wooded incline. Eventually, in order to facilitate expansion, a few roads were cut into it, and new subdivisions were built on the high ground overlooking the original settlement.

Dawn lived in the old part of town. Her two best friends, Peggy and Starr, lived in the new—in adjacent subdivisions, in fact—near the high school, which perched on the very edge of the escarpment. To visit Dawn, Peggy and Starr usually followed an old Indian trail down a rugged canyon, which terminated at the edge of Landa Park near those springs that were the source of the Comal River. From the park they would then make a shortcut through the railroad switching yard to Seguin Street, which, in turn, led through downtown and into Dawn's neighborhood.

On Saturday morning they reached the Ramsey home at 9:30 and found Helen Ramsey rushing about madly, trying to get ready for work. Normally she did not go in to her job on weekends, but this morning her employer had been taken ill, and she, as assistant manager, would have to open in his place. Bleary eyed and still in her nightie, Dawn was ironing a dress for Meghan, who was dawdling over a bowl of Cheerios.

"What can we do to help?" Starr offered.

"Finish ironing this for me," Dawn suggested. "Maybe I can hurry Meghan up by feeding her."

"I'm not a baby," Meghan protested. "I can feed myself."

"Well, you're not doing it, are you?" Dawn snapped. "Come on now. Let's pretend you're the queen and I'm your maid servant. Open wide."

Meghan obstinately clamped her mouth shut.

Sleep deprived, Dawn was not in any mood to be patient. "Mom's leaving in less than ten minutes, and you're going with her whether or not you've had a single bite to eat. So be as stubborn as you want. I don't care."

Peggy stepped forward and curtseyed to Meghan. "Your majesty, would you permit me to feed you?"

Meghan nodded her consent, and Peggy took the spoon from Dawn and began shoveling Cheerios into Meghan's open mouth. Meghan, because the cereal was already so soggy, did not even bother to chew, but simply swallowed one bite after another until the bowl was empty. Dawn was standing by with a damp wash cloth and immediately wiped her little sister's face. Then Starr put the freshly ironed dress over Meghan's head, buttoned it up the back, and tied her sash.

"Thanks for all the help girls," said Ms Ramsey. "Have fun today, and be good. I'll see you at 6:30 tonight."

"How come you're not dressed yet?" Peggy asked Dawn when Ms Ramsey and Meghan were away.

"Overslept, I guess. Last night I couldn't fall asleep for thinking about what we were going to do today, and this morning I almost couldn't wake up."

Whilst Peggy and Starr washed the Ramseys' breakfast dishes and cleaned the kitchen, Dawn put on shorts and a polo shirt.

Even though the month was February, the temperature was in the mid 70s. Mild winters were one of the most-agreeable advantages to living in this part of Texas.

The three girls found Leo sitting on his front porch sipping coffee. Dawn made proper introductions. Then Leo invited them inside for a breakfast of crumpets, strawberries and kiwi fruit, and hot cocoa. Long after the food was gone, the four of them continued to sit around the table talking, laughing, and joking. Peggy and Starr had taken an

51

immediate liking to Leo, and he was finding them totally delightful.

Eventually, though, the task of painting the tree house could be put off no longer. Leo supplied painting smocks in the form of old tattered shirts of his. The girls put them on over their own clothes and buttoned them up to the necks. Dawn in shorts and Starr in a miniskirt had only to remove their shoes and socks in order to be adequately protected. Peggy, however, was wearing blue jeans, and Leo was afraid that she would get paint on the lower legs of them.

"I can take them off," she offered. "This big old shirt is like a dress on me anyway."

"I do think that would be better," Leo agreed. "Do you want to go into the bathroom to change?"

"Not really," said Peggy, hiking up her oversize shirt, unzipping her jeans, and shimmying out of them. "See? I'm already done."

Outside, Leo demonstrated the proper technique for applying paint, gave each of the three a brush of her own, then carried the open paint buckets up for them. The colors to be employed were cream for the walls, dusty rose and antique lavender for the gingerbread trim and the safety rail, and dark green for the shutters and the door. As they worked, Leo sat on the back stairs making sketches of them. Shortly Mercy emerged from her apartment, walked back the driveway, and opened the garage doors. When she noticed Leo on the back stairs, she came over to see what he was working on.

"Hi, Mercy!" Dawn shouted and waved from the deck of the tree house.

Mercy waved back.

"What are you up to this morning?" Leo asked.

"I have shopping to do. My niece in Houston is having a birthday soon. I want to send her a nice

52

present. If I can't find what I want here, I may drive down to San Antonio or up to San Marcos. Can I pick up anything for you?"

"I could use a few more drawing pads like this one." Leo showed her the cover. "But only if you're near an art-supply store. Don't go out of your way."

"*Strathmore*," she read. "I'll get them. Anything else?"

"That's all," said Leo, getting to his feet and reaching a hand into his pocket. "Let me give you some money."

"Later. I'll bring you a receipt, and you can pay me then."

Not long after Mercy left, Christi came out and drove away in her own car.

By noon the girls were very nearly through painting. Leo asked them what they would like for lunch. He had prepared nothing, but intended to send out. So they could have anything that could be delivered. They considered hamburgers, barbecue, and Chinese food, but settled, instead, on pizza. Then of course, there was a huge debate as to what toppings to ask for. Eventually Leo was able to phone an order in, and it was delivered by Robyn of the red hair.

"Have you changed jobs?" he asked as he counted out the money. "Didn't you work for the bakery?"

"Still do. This is my second job."

"How many jobs do you have?"

"Three. On Friday and Saturday nights, I take tickets at the Lone Star Ballroom. Do you ever go dancing?"

"Not there. I don't do the Texas two-step."

"You could learn," she teased. "It's fun."

"That's just it, Robyn. I'm not really into fun. Fun, it seems to me, is at best a poor substitute for pleasure."

"Mmm," Robyn mused, "I never thought of it that way, but you're right."

"And speaking of pleasure, when am I going to get to paint you again?"

"Probably never. With three jobs, I don't have any time left over for the things I enjoy."

"Then why do it?"

"I've decided to go to college. I'm trying to sock away all I can before the summer term starts."

Leo added five dollars to her tip. "Smart girl. I admire your ambition."

"Thanks. And take care. I have to run."

From the tree house, Dawn called to Leo, "We're almost done, but not quite. Can you keep that pizza warm for a little while?"

Twenty minutes later, the girls climbed down the rope ladder and began washing their brushes at an outdoor faucet. Leo brought them a bottle of liquid detergent to use. When their brushes were clean, they started working at getting the paint off their hands, arms, legs, and faces. Thankfully, none had paint in her hair. At Leo's suggestion they stripped off their smocks and laid them out on the lawn to dry. Leo had quite forgotten that Peggy had earlier removed her jeans, and so too, apparently, had Peggy forgotten. In only her panties and blouse, she entered the studio behind the other two girls.

"Is everyone completely clean?" Leo asked. "Are you certain that all the paint is off you?"

"We checked one another out carefully," Peggy assured him.

"Oh, my!" exclaimed Leo, noticing for the first time Peggy's state of undress. I'm sorry I told you to take that smock off outside. I didn't remember till just now that you didn't have pants on under it."

"That's okay," Peggy answered. "Your backyard is very private. Nobody could see me."

"Then why don't you put your jeans on now?" Leo suggested.

As Starr and Dawn went through the pantry to the kitchen in order to put out the pizza and open sodas, Peggy walked to the far end of the studio, where she had left her jeans. The backs of her legs, Leo noticed, were crisscrossed with angry red welts. In places the skin was actually broken, and scabs were starting to form.

"Peggy," Leo said softly, "did someone beat you with a strap?"

Tears immediately formed in Peggy's eyes, and her lower lip began to tremble. "I don't want to talk about it. Please, just forget it."

"Tell me what happened," Leo insisted

Peggy shook her head and refused to answer.

"Who did this, Peggy? You have to tell me that much. I'm not going to let it go until you do."

"It was my own fault. I knew what would happen."

"Who beat you? Was it your father?"

Peggy's nod of assent was barely perceptible.

Leo was horrified, but he was unsure how to proceed. "I ought to call the police or social services or somebody, but I'm afraid they might be more interested to know how I happened to see you without your pants."

"Then let's not tell anybody," Peggy suggested. "It wouldn't do any good anyway."

"I'm going to talk to my friend Mercy, who lives upstairs. You haven't met her yet, but Dawn knows her well. She's someone you can trust.  She knows lots of people, and she knows how things work here."

"You're going to get me in worse trouble than I've ever been in.  I don't need anybody to help me."

"Don't worry, Peggy.  We won't take any steps without your permission.  But we have to figure out what's possible."

"You won't tell anybody else?"

"I promise."

"Hey, you guys!" Dawn called from the kitchen. "Pizza's getting cold.  Are you coming or what?"

"Go ahead and put your jeans on," Leo instructed Peggy.  "I'm famished, aren't you?"

# VII
## PEGGY

A t the Christian bookstore, Mercy selected a pen-and-pencil set, a box of stationery, a beautifully bound book of blank pages, and a birthday card, then idly browsed the book shelves until Helen Ramsey replaced another clerk at the check-out counter.

"Do you gift-wrap?" Mercy asked as Helen rang up her purchases.

"Gladly."

"You're Helen Ramsey, aren't you? I thought I recognized you when I came in."

"That's right. And you look familiar too, but I can't place you."

"I'm Mercy Gruenewald. I used to work at the library in San Antonio."

"Of course! I remember. So good to see you again. What brings you all the way out to New Braunfels?"

"I live here now. And you?"

"We moved up here almost six years ago. We love it."

"And how is Dawn?" Mercy inquired. "That is your daughter's name, is it not?"

"That's right. She's a big girl now. You wouldn't know her. She's just had her eleventh birthday."

"Still a book lover?"

"Yes, she's a voracious reader," Helen said, "and very independent. No one can tell her anything."

"She's her own person, you mean? That's good."

Helen was not so sure. "Sometimes it's hard to believe that she's a child of mine. I love her with all my heart, but I do wish she weren't so rebellious."

Mercy patted Helen's hand sympathetically. "You have to let her make her own choices. That's the most difficult part of being a parent, I should imagine."

"You don't have children then?"

Mercy shook her head sadly. "When I was younger, I desperately wanted to have a baby, but it was never convenient. And now I'm no longer married. So I pamper my only niece and my many honorary nieces. I encourage their creativity and support them in all their undertakings. I get to enjoy them without having to discipline them or go through any unpleasantness with them. I guess I have the ideal arrangement. But I'd still like to be a mother."

From New Braunfels Mercy drove north to San Marcos, where she bought Leo the drawing pads he wanted and herself a variety of craft supplies. She was fond of dabbling in ceramics, cross-stitch, flower-pressing, and scrapbooking. On the return trip, she stopped for lunch at a Pig & Whistle barbecue stand.

Meanwhile Leo and the girls were finishing off their pizza.

"Leo," said Starr, "I know the tree house is really for your granddaughter, but until she comes, would it be okay for the three of us to use it once in a while?"

"Sorry, Starr," Leo told her. "I just let you do all that work for nothing."

"Oh, I see." Starr was clearly disappointed, but determined to be a good sport nonetheless.

Dawn shoved her playfully. "You dunce! Can't you tell he's joking?"

"You mean it really is okay for us to use it?"

"Any time," Leo assured her, "and as often as you wish, even if I'm not here."

"Should we check with Mercy first?" Dawn asked for clarification.

"No need for that. She and I are in complete agreement about this. Just consider the tree house your own."

All three girls squealed with pleasure and heaped copious thanks on Leo. Dawn even hugged him and kissed his cheek.

"Yoo-hoo! Anybody home?" Mercy was calling from the back door.

Dawn hopped up and ran to let her in.

"I bumped into your mother this morning," said Mercy, entering the studio.

Dawn felt weak in the knees. "You didn't tell her I've been coming over here without permission, did you?"

"I didn't even mention having seen you recently." Mercy placed the newly purchased drawing pads on Leo's desk. "I merely laid the groundwork for inviting you to come play with my niece the next time she's in town."

Dawn was impressed. "That was pretty smart. Thank you."

"I've been showing your pamphlets around, and I've found a couple of booksellers—one in Austin and one in San Marcos—who are willing to display your literature in their stores. You'll have to set prices for everything."

"Are you serious? This is too unbelievable! I was afraid nobody would want to read what I published and people would think I was silly for going to all that trouble."

"I doubt that anyone will think you silly. Rationalists, like myself, cannot but admire you. And even Christian fundamentalists must respect you as a formidable foe."

"I don't want to be anybody's foe. I'm only the foe of stupidity and superstition."

"Well said, child. Well said."

"Mercy, I need to ask your advice about something. How hard do you think it would be for me to start up a little magazine? Pamphlets were just the beginning. Eventually I intend to publish books, but that can wait till later. For now, I've got this idea for a really neat quarterly journal. Would that even be possible?"

"Something on the scale of a newsletter might not be too difficult or too expensive. Can you come up with enough material every three months?"

"Not by myself, but maybe I could get my two best friends to help; and I'm pretty sure the three of us together can write enough articles, at least to begin with. Once we're established, our readers will probably send us articles to publish, don't you think?"

"I couldn't say. But if there's anybody in the world who can pull this off, Dawn, that person is you."

"I've been trying to think of the perfect way to put this to my friends, so they'll understand what a good plan it is. But every time I start to tell them, I change my mind, because I'm afraid they'll say no."

"You'll find the right way, I'm sure. Now, let's go on in, and you can introduce them to me."

At Mercy's invitation Peggy, Dawn, and Starr trouped upstairs to plunder through a box of old curtains in search of some that might fit the windows of the tree house. Predictably, each of the girls favored a different set, but eventually, after considerable wrangling, a compromise was reached. The curtains not to be used were neatly refolded and returned to the box, and the box was put away. An extensive search then ensued for curtain rods. Mercy was almost certain that she had some extras somewhere, but they were not to be found. So she gave the girls money and sent them downtown to buy new ones. They were gone for less than an hour.

Upon their return, they were met in the front yard by Leo, who offered to help them hang their curtains.

"Thanks," said Dawn, "but first, I have to pee."

"Me too," said Starr.

Leo took the new curtain rods from them and instructed them to use either of the bathrooms in his apartment. "Peggy and I shall meet you at the tree house when you're done."

Peggy started after her two friends. "I've got to pee too."

"Wait, Peggy. You can use the bathroom in Mercy's apartment. She needs to have a word with you in private."

In the living room of the upstairs apartment, Peggy found both Mercy and Christi waiting for her, and immediately preempted any conversation by asking permission to use the bathroom. When she came out, Mercy motioned for her to sit beside her on the sofa. Reluctantly Peggy did as bade.

"This is my friend Christi. She's a nurse. We want to see the marks on your legs. If they're as bad as Leo says, I'm going to take some pictures, and I need Christi to be my witness."

Peggy had known that this was coming, but she was still upset. "You weren't supposed to tell anybody else. Leo promised."

"Christi has no official status, Peggy. She's not with the police, and she's not with Children's Protective Services. What's more, she doesn't even know who you are. I haven't told her your last name. Leo's promise binds both of us as well. Unless you say so, this will go no further."

"Then why bother? Because I'm not going to say so."

Christi explained. "It's evidence, sweetie. We may never be able to use these pictures, but on the other hand, if you're trying someday to do something about your situation, it'll help to have this proof of physical abuse."

"Just in case," Mercy added. "Think of it this way: as insurance against what may happen in the future. If you're prepared, you'll stand a better chance of winning should the day ever come when you have to fight for yourself."

"Alright, I guess. But you won't do anything else unless I agree, right?"

Christi and Mercy both swore solemnly. Peggy removed first her jeans and then her blouse. Mercy made a series of digital photographs. Worse even than the welts and cuts on Peggy's legs were purple and yellow bruises on her shoulders and ribs.

"Sometimes he uses a rod instead of a belt," Peggy explained. "It's biblical."

Mercy went to the desk in her bedroom and printed full-sheet enlargements of all the pictures she had taken.

Left alone briefly with Peggy, who was getting dressed again, Christi told her, "I used to be a school nurse. I've been through this before with other kids, and I probably shouldn't say this, but you're absolutely right to be afraid of reporting what's been going on. Too often mistreated children end up right back in the custody of the parents who hurt them. However, if your life becomes unendurable, you may have to take your chances with the system, because sometimes it does work. And always remember, you have friends in Leo and Mercy and me."

As previously arranged, Peggy and Starr spent that night with Dawn, then accompanied the Ramseys to church the next morning, where they rejoined their own families. Dawn spent Sunday afternoon reading aloud to Meghan. Consequently, she was hoarse the next day when she called on Leo.

"What's happened to your voice?" he asked as he showed her in.

"I guess I've been talking too much lately," she croaked.

"May I offer you a bite to eat?"

Dawn nodded vigorously. She was famished.

"Pasta salad, garlic toast, and iced tea," Leo suggested. "How does that sound?"

Dawn nodded again. She meant to save her voice as much as possible.

Whilst Leo prepared her snack, Dawn walked out to the studio to see what he might have painted since Saturday. On the easel was an unfinished nude portrait of a young woman Dawn recognized as a grocery clerk at the HEB, and on the floor beneath the windows, leaning against the north wall, was a landscape of the cliffs along the Guadalupe River. Of greater interest to her than either of these paintings was a neatly typed essay on the desk. She picked it up, but read only the title:

The Liberal Alternative

Back in the kitchen, she asked in a whisper, "What's this for?"

Leo glanced over his shoulder to see what she was talking about. "Oh, that. It's a short homily to be read next week at a gathering of religious humanists in Cibolo. My daughter is in charge of the program. She asked me to participate in a small way."

"What's a homily?"

"A homily is a sermon. Of course, this one is very short, and in no way like any sermon you would hear in a Christian church."

"May I read it?"

"Sure. But don't you want to eat first. This will be ready by the time you can set the table."

# VIII
## Evidence of Abuse

M ercy furnished the tree house with an area rug, a child-size table-and-chair set, throw pillows for the built-in window seats, and one small bookcase, which soon overflowed with books borrowed from Leo and from Mercy.

Leo had more than two thousand volumes in his apartment, and Mercy had about the same number. Both adults encouraged all the children of their acquaintance to read any of these works that appealed to them. Subject matter ranged from history and biography to arts and crafts and included anthropology, poetry, fiction, and philosophy. Thus it was that Dawn discovered and fell in love with the works of Marcus Aurelius, Bertrand Russell, Robert Ingersoll, Will Durant, Edward Gibbon, Lao-tzu, and Corliss Lamont, whom she mistakenly referred to once as *Lamont Cranston*, evoking amused smiles from both Mercy and Leo. Leo tactfully corrected her and explained who Lamont Cranston was supposed to have been. Dawn was mortified by her error, but thankful to be put straight.

Only once did Leo refuse to loan her a book. It was the explicitly illustrated *Joy of Sex* by Dr Alex Comfort. "Personally, Dawn, I don't object to your reading this, but I'm afraid of the repercussions should it ever be learned that I allowed you to do so."

"Leo," Dawn reminded him, "you know I never tell my parents anything. They don't even know that you exist."

"Nevertheless, I would prefer that we both pretend that I am unaware that you are looking at this particular book. Don't take it to the tree house, and don't have it open whilst I am in the room."

"Okay, I can live with that. Thanks."

Throughout the remainder of the winter, Dawn called on Leo every weekday after school and as frequently on Saturdays as she could manage. As much as she loved reading books, she loved discussing them with someone knowledgeable and interested in the same sort of ideas that intrigued her. Leo's own personal journal, *Observations and Contemplations*, soon became her favorite literary work in the entire world, for in it he dealt sensibly with every significant issue relevant to the human condition.

Leo, for his part, so looked forward to Dawn's visits that he made it a special point to be at home whenever she could reasonably be expected to show up. Sundays, of course, she was required to spend with her family.

Leo saw Peggy and Starr less often. They occasionally came on Saturdays with Dawn; and once on a Sunday afternoon, Peggy, quite alone, knocked on Leo's door, her face smeared with blood.

Leo was appalled. "Come in, Peggy. What on earth has happened to you?"

"It's nothing much. I've had worse."

In the front bathroom, Leo had Peggy sit on the side of the tub whilst he gently washed her face. Most of the blood had come from her nostrils, but her lower lip was split as well.

"Did your father do this to you?" Leo asked, applying salve to the visible wound.

"It was my own fault. I knew better than to say what I said."

"Tell me what happened," Leo coaxed.

"We were at the dinner table. He wanted me to say grace, which I never do. I don't know why he keeps asking me. But anyway, after I refused, he went ahead and did it himself; he prayed and prayed and prayed till our food got cold. I guess I should have done it, because I wouldn't have been so long-winded. By the time he finished, I was in a really foul mood, and that's why I told him that he was disobeying the Bible, because Jesus said to go into a closet to pray, where only God can hear you."

"It looks as if he hit you with his fist."

Peggy shook her head. "The back of his hand. My chair turned over, and I hit my head on the corner of the hutch."

"Show me."

Peggy twisted around and put her hand on the back of her skull; then with her fingertips, she parted her hair to reveal another nasty cut, upon which Leo smeared antibiotic ointment.

"Are you going to get Mercy to take more pictures?"

"I should really like to, but Mercy's in Houston for the weekend, and I don't have a camera myself. Maybe—"

"Maybe what?"

"I do have a key to Mercy's apartment. Maybe I can find her camera and figure out how to use it."

"I know where she keeps it," Peggy told him, "and I can teach you how to use it."

Leo snapped half a dozen exposures, all of which came out sharp and clear. He only regretted that he had cleaned the blood from Peggy's face before photographing her. Gory images would have been so much more compelling.

"Did you get any lunch?" Leo asked as they walked back to his apartment.

"A couple of bites, that's all."

"Would you like a sandwich?"

Peggy nodded. "I'm starved."

"We should try to get that blood out of your dress before it's too late to do anything about it."

"My mother always says blood's tricky to get out. Do you know how?"

"Yes, I think so."

As they entered the apartment, Peggy started unbuttoning the back of her dress.

"Wait, Peggy," Leo hurried to say. "I want you to go into the bathroom to undress, but first let's find something for you to put on. Imagine what someone might think who came to my door and saw you here only partially clad."

"I'm sorry," Peggy apologized. "I wasn't thinking."

In fact, no callers were expected and none came. Peggy put on one of Leo's starched dress shirts and ate her sandwich at the breakfast table whilst at the kitchen sink Leo worked on the blood stains. Later, when he had hung the dress out of doors to dry, they sat together in the living room and chatted until late in the day.

70

# IX

## BERYL

I n early March Leo's daughter Carmen was badly injured in an automobile collision; so Leo went to San Antonio to help look after his granddaughter Brenda during Carmen's hospitalization and recuperation. He had not time to tell Dawn that he was leaving, but asked Mercy to tell her for him.

With Leo away, Dawn began visiting Mercy after school every weekday. The two of them soon became close confidants.

"My niece from Houston is coming for spring break," Mercy told Dawn one afternoon. "I'm going to ask your mother if it's okay to invite you over to meet her. You're here every day anyway, but without your parents' knowledge or permission. You're risking big trouble, I think."

"I think so too," Dawn agreed, "but it's worth it."

"Well, I'm hoping to legitimize your visits. You don't mind, do you?"

"No, that's a good plan."

Beryl Gruenewald was almost two years Dawn's senior, but so diminutive of stature that no one would have guessed her true age. Mercy filled Beryl in on Dawn's situation before taking her to the bookstore to meet Helen Ramsey and to extend an invitation for Dawn to dine with them that evening.

Dawn and Beryl hit it off immediately. With the Ramseys' blessing, Dawn spent every waking minute of her vacation in Beryl's company. At the end of the week, Peggy and Starr joined them as well.

On Friday afternoon in the tree house, the Little Heathens' Underground Tract Society and Free

71

Press was chartered.   To sign in blood an oath of secrecy, all four girls pricked their thumbs with a needle.  Starr fainted, but Dawn and Beryl caught her and eased her to the floor.   Peggy ran inside for a damp washcloth to put on Starr's forehead, but when she returned, she found Starr already revived.   The next order of business was creation of job titles and aliases for every member of the group.   Dawn as *Dusky Nightshade* would be publisher; Starr as *Ouida Peeples* would be editress-in-chief; Peggy as *Pagan Wright* would be associate editress; and Beryl as *Kelly Greene* would be art directress. Later Mercy served them refreshments at her dining-room table.   Then the girls returned to the tree house for a brainstorming session to come up with a list of topics to be written about.   Assignments were made, and deadlines were set.

"At last!" Dawn exclaimed.   "Now we truly are in business."

There was just one thing Beryl wanted to know. "How are we going to pay for all this?"

Dawn assured her and the others that none of them would be asked to put money into the project. "I'm paying for everything out of my allowance and with my savings."

Beryl returned to Houston on Sunday afternoon, but promised to stay in touch by "snail mail," since Dawn had no email account and no cell phone.

# X

## BRENDA

The following Friday night, Leo rode the bus back to New Braunfels, his granddaughter Brenda in tow. She was to spend the weekend with him. One or both of her parents would collect her on Sunday afternoon and drive her home.

At 9:00 that evening, Mercy telephoned Helen Ramsey to say that one of her honorary nieces—her neighbor's granddaughter actually—was in town for the next two days. "She has no friends here; so I was hoping Dawn might want to hang out with her tomorrow."

"That's fine by me," Helen said, "but Dawn's already gone to bed tonight. I'll tell her in the morning. Can she call you then?"

"That'll be fine. Do you need my number again?"

"I still have it. But on second thought, let me suggest a different plan. Perhaps Brenda would like to have breakfast with us in the morning. I've already promised the girls that I'll make pancakes."

"Brenda's favorite. What time shall I have her there?"

Brenda was the same age as Peggy. She was sweet, polite, and biddable. Dawn could hardly imagine that she had any opinion whatever on those issues that she herself considered vital. Dawn had looked forward to Brenda's being an important addition to her tract society, but now she doubted that Brenda could be enticed to participate in such a subversive enterprise. Brenda was simply too well adjusted.

Helen Ramsey, on the other hand, totally approved of Brenda as a friend and companion for her elder daughter. She even took it upon herself to invite Brenda to come back tonight for a sleep-over. Brenda thought that sounded like a lot of fun, but unfortunately, she already had plans to camp out in her new tree house tonight. Maybe Dawn could sleep over with her there.

"Uh—well," Helen stammered. "Sure, I don't see why not. I'll call your aunt later in the day, and we can work out the details."

Brenda was momentarily at a loss. "My aunt?"

"I mean Mercy," Helen explained. "She referred to you as an honorary niece, and I just forgot that it was only honorary."

"Oh, yes, now I see. She's told me lots of times to call her *Aunt Mercy*, but I never can remember to."

After breakfast Dawn and Brenda walked hand in hand to Leo's apartment. But when Dawn saw Leo in the yard, she released Brenda's hand and ran to him, threw her arms about his neck, and kissed his cheek.

"I take it you're glad to see me," Leo chuckled.

"I've never missed anybody as much in my whole life. If you go away again, take me with you."

"Your parents might have something to say about that."

"They'd probably be relieved,"

"Don't you believe it," Leo chided. "Mercy tells me that you're mother is very nice and loves you a lot."

"That's true," Dawn conceded. "She's even going to let me spend the night in the tree house with Brenda."

Surprised, Leo glanced at Brenda, as if for confirmation.

Brenda smiled guiltily. "I invited her. Is that okay?"

"It's fine. I'm just amazed that Dawn's mother agreed. She tends to be a bit overprotective. You must have made a very good impression."

"All I did was mind my manners, like you said, 'Uelo, and not mention you at all."

"How come you call him *Waylo*?" Dawn asked Brenda.

Brenda shrugged her shoulders. "I don't know. It's just what I've always called him."

"*Abuelo* is the Spanish word for *grandfather*," Leo explained. "She just drops the first syllable."

75

Dawn was still puzzled. "But you're not Spanish, are you?"

"Cuban," Leo told her.

Now Dawn was totally perplexed. "I thought you were British."

"I lived in England for many years. My daughter was born there. Brenda was born there. And these days I travel on a British passport, but I was born in Cuba. My family, you see, were visiting in London when the Revolution came. We could never go home."

"Then is *Madrigal* a Spanish name?"

"Absolutely. Now, what are you two planning for today?"

"I don't know," said Dawn. "Whatever Brenda wants to do is fine with me."

"How about if we just go downtown and look around?"

"That sounds fun. I go window-shopping a lot."

"Will you be back for lunch?" Leo asked Brenda. "Or would you like some money to eat out?"

"If it wouldn't cost too much, maybe we could eat at that drugstore where you took me last time."

Leo reached into his pocket and gave Brenda a twenty-dollar bill. "This should be more than enough for both of you."

Thank you, 'Uelo. I'll bring you back the extra."

Leo waved his hand dismissively. "Just hang onto it. It's always nice to have a little pocket change."

It would have been impossible for Dawn not to like Brenda, for not only was Brenda always pleasant and agreeable, she practically worshiped Dawn and would have done almost anything to please her.

"Do you, by any chance," Dawn ventured, "know how to compose a really good essay?"

"What's an essay?"

"Like a paper you have to write for school. You've done that before, haven't you?"

"I did a research paper on zebras once. Why?"

Dawn told Brenda about her newly formed club and about the periodical they planned soon to start publishing. "You can be a member if you want. I'll teach you how to write an essay, or else we can find some other job for you to do."

"Will I get to have a secret identity?"

"Well, sure. How about *Bunny O'Hare*?"

Brenda stuck a finger down her throat as if to gag herself.

"Well, you could be *Stormy Knight*."

"That's a pretty good one, but I'd like to try to think of one myself."

"Okay, but if you don't ever write any essays for us to publish," Dawn pointed out, "you won't really need one anyway."

"Don't worry. I'm going to knock your socks off."

Brenda had not the native talent for writing that Dawn had. Nor had she the advantage of having had an outstanding composition teacher. What she possessed (and in spades) was bull-headed determination that would not allow her to quit trying until she had produced at least one publishable essay. The easiest forms for her to master were comparisons and contrasts. Her first successful effort was entitled "Knowing and Believing." The *nom de plume* she chose for herself was *Wendy March*.

Upon receipt of Brenda's submission, Dawn wrote a letter of congratulations, praising her so highly that Brenda was persuaded to continue writing, even though the process remained excruciating to her.

Beryl, on the other hand, seemed to have forgotten all about her literary commitments. Weeks passed with no word from her. Dawn was especially disappointed, since she had entertained such high hopes for what Beryl might contribute. The alibi furnished by Mercy was that Beryl had a new boyfriend. "He's all that she can think about at the moment. Just give her a little time, and I'm sure you'll hear from her."

"I'm not going to worry about it," Dawn swore. "It's Starr's job to come up with enough material to fill the pages. But what am I going to do for an address?"

"What do you mean?" Mercy asked.

"My publishing company has to have an address if I'm going to get people to subscribe or submit articles or send letters to the editress. I can't use my own address, or everybody will know that I'm *Dusky Nightshade*. And I can't use the address of any of my friends either. Best would be an out-of-town address, and not Beryl's or Brenda's, because my mom would recognize it for sure."

"Then what about Christi's address. She's in Houston now."

"Is it a permanent address?"

"She may not stay long in the apartment she's in, but she does expect to remain in Houston, and she receives her mail at a post-office box."

"Perfect. Do you think she'd mind?"

"I'm sure she wouldn't. I'll call her tonight."

I ssue Number One of *Dusky Nightshade's Opuscule* was almost ready for printing. It was shy only the single article that had been expected from Beryl. In her capacity as editress-in-chief, Starr, desperate for a little extra material, asked Leo whether he might have anything she could use to fill the blank space.

"You mean something I've written myself?"

"Sure. Why not? Dawn told me she read a little sermonette you wrote once, and it was really good."

"Actually, I've written several. You're welcome to use any of them you like. But I'm wondering whether your credibility might not suffer by your not writing all the articles yourselves."

"I don't see why it would. We've already decided to use professional clip art and put in quotes by famous authors. Also, we're asking our readers to submit articles, and that means all our readers, not just the ones under a certain age."

# XI
## TOBY TO THE RESCUE

Peggy, meanwhile, was facing more difficulties than just an abusive father. For some inexplicable reason, a band of neighborhood thugs had singled her out for singular persecution. These were public-school seventh-grade boys, whose leader was grossly overweight Junior Weeks. Junior always called Peggy *KJV*. She had no idea why, but refused to ask. She would never give him the satisfaction of imagining that she spent even a second wondering about it. Indeed, Peggy always did her best to ignore Junior and his goons. Unfortunately, they refused to be completely ignored. Whenever they caught Peggy leaving her house afoot and alone, they followed, crowding around obnoxiously close, talking crudely about her amongst themselves.

"What color panties do you think she has on today?" Junior asked one afternoon as Peggy walked to the 7-Eleven on an errand for her mother.

Each of Junior's three companions guessed a different color.

"Nope, you're all wrong," Junior told them. "KJV only wears white panties. Isn't that right, KJV?"

Peggy did not respond in any way whatever, but continued walking as briskly as she could. What Junior had said was actually true. But how, she wondered, could Junior possibly know that the only undergarments her mother ever bought her or allowed her to own were of plain white cotton and innocent of any unnecessary frills, such as ruffles or ribbons? Did the whole world know?

"Want to know why?" Junior asked.  Then without waiting for a reply, he revealed the secret. "White represents her purity."

"What make you so sure she's still pure?" pimply-faced Rodney Sparks sniggered.

"She's a preacher's kid," Junior reasoned. "She has to be good.  Ain't that right, KJV?  Hey! Want to know why we call you that.  I thought you'd never ask.  KJV stands for King James Virgin.  You are a virgin, aren't you?  'Cause that's a condition I'd be happy to remedy for you."

Peggy halted momentarily and turned to shout in Junior's face.  "I'm ten years old, Junior.  I'm in fourth grade. So fuck off!  Go bother somebody else for a change."

"No can do, KJV.  We like you, even if you don't like us."

Peggy shook her head in frustration as she walked away.

"Show us your panties," Shorty Schneider urged her. "I'll bet you guys ten dollars they ain't white."

"And I'll bet twenty she ain't no virgin neither," bucktoothed Billy Bunton sneered.  "Her old man probably knocked her off hisself."

"No way," Junior said.  "She's been saving it for us—well—for me, that is.  But I'll let you guys have sloppy seconds."

The taunts continued.  Peggy, even though she was near to panic, marched stoically onward. Suddenly she felt her skirt being lifted from behind.

"See?" Junior crowed.  "White panties, just like I told you.  She's as pure as rain water."

Peggy had had all that she could take.  She bolted for the relative safety of the 7-Eleven, which was now in sight. As she ran, tears of rage coursed down her cheeks. She was not pursued, but she knew that she must encounter her tormentors again on the way home, and she was filled with dread.

Now, there happened also to live in Peggy's neighborhood a ninth-grade boy named Toby Faust, who seemed always to go out of his way to say hello to Peggy or at least to smile and wave. She had never had an actual conversation with him, but she knew that he liked her, and she certainly liked him. What girl would not? As luck would have it, Toby was at the 7-Eleven that day, and when Peggy explained her predicament, he readily agreed to walk her home after her shopping was done. He even carried her groceries for her. They saw nothing of Junior's gang along the way.

A few days later, however, as Peggy was coming home from Starr's house at suppertime, she found herself once more surrounded by her usual antagonists.

"Hello there, KJV," Junior called out cheerily. "Listen, I want to apologize for the other day. We got a little too rowdy with you, but we didn't mean no harm. You know, the only reason we tease you is that we're so fond of you."

Peggy rolled her eyes in exasperation and tried unsuccessfully to push her way past Junior, who had planted himself squarely in her path.

"I'm serious, KJV. I've decided to turn over a new leaf. No more teasing."

"Yeah," Rodney leered, "from now on, we're as serious as a heart attack. So who you want to go into the bushes with first?"

"Shut up that kind of talk!" Junior scolded. "I'm trying to do the right thing by this poor girl, and all you can think about is getting her onto her back."

Rodney looked as if he had been slapped. "Sorry, KJV. I didn't mean nothing."

Junior was still blocking Peggy's way. "You're probably in a hurry, right?"

"You could say that," Peggy agreed.

"Well, just answer me this one question, and you can go. It's something I've been wondering about for three or four months now."

"What's that, Junior? Let's get this over with."

"Is your heart a radio?"

"What?" Peggy was not even sure that she had understood the question correctly.

"Do you have a radio in your chest?" Junior pronounced the words slowly and clearly. "I have to know."

"Of course not. Now get out of my way."

"Then what are these two little knobs for?" And so saying, Junior put his hands to Peggy's chest and roughly tweaked her developing breast buds.

Infuriated and in considerable pain, Peggy reacted by kneeing Junior in the crotch, and when he doubled over in agony, she socked him in the face with her fist. He stumbled backward, tripped over the curb, and fell to the ground. Peggy ran for her life as Junior's three buddies collapsed in laughter.

"Get up, you idiots!" Junior shouted. "Cut her off."

The three fanned out to prevent Peggy's getting out of the immediate neighborhood as Junior hauled himself to his feet and set out in close pursuit of her. Peggy, realizing the hopelessness of her situation, dashed toward the only sanctuary she could think of, the Faust residence. If Toby were not at home, there would be no way for her to avoid whatever vengeance Junior meant to extract.

But happily, Toby was at home. In fact, he was in the driveway changing a bicycle tire. He looked up and saw Peggy, terrified for her life, running toward him with Junior lumbering after her. Toby got to his feet and stepped out into the street to meet her, and she clung to him, too out of breath to speak.

"You're safe now. I'll take care of this."

Momentum carried Junior onward, even after he realized that the tables had been turned. When he was able to stop running, he found himself face to face with his nemesis. Toby abused him for a coward and slapped his face repeatedly, then required him to kneel at Peggy's feet and beg her forgiveness.

Peggy bent and whispered in Junior's ear, "If you or any of your stupid friends so much as look at me ever again as long as you live, I'll personally cut your penis off while Toby holds you down. Do you believe me?"

Pale as a sheet, Junior nodded.

"Get out of here," Toby told him. "And don't ever bother her again."

As Junior loped away, Toby asked Peggy what she had whispered in Junior's ear.

"A Bible verse," she lied glibly, "something to help him become a better person."

Toby laughed. "I might have expected something like that from a preacher's kid."

# XII
## Damien Wynter

Starr finished laying out the first issue of *Opuscule* on a Thursday, copied it to an SD card, and passed the card to Dawn before classes commenced the next day. Dawn printed all the pages front-to-back that afternoon when she got home from school, then carried them in a cardboard box to the tree house, where Starr and Peggy were to help her assemble them on Saturday. Of course, Dawn did take the time to put together one complete copy to present to Leo. She simply could not wait until tomorrow for him to see what she had wrought.

She knocked first at Leo's back door and got no response; so she went to the front door and rang the bell. Whilst she waited for Leo to come let her in, Damien walked up behind her.

"'Rosy-fingered Dawn,' how's the world been treating you?"

Startled, Dawn jumped. "Oh, Mr Wynter, you nearly scared the snot out of me."

"Sorry, I thought you saw me when I drove up."

Dawn denied it. "I'm really glad you're here though. I have a present for you, but first you have to promise to keep my secret."

"Wonderful! If there's anything I like as much as a present, it's a secret."

They were interrupted then by Leo's unlatching the screen door. "Did you two arrive together?"

Dawn entered first. "No, we just met right here. What took you so long to come to the door? And why are you wearing an apron?"

"Are you baking?" Damien asked Leo as he followed Dawn inside. "You have flour on your face."

85

"I'm making scones," Leo explained. "I've been yearning for some, and the bakery never seems to have them."

Dawn and Damien seated themselves at the dining table as Leo set about preparing tea.

"Mr Wynter," Dawn asked, "may I borrow your pen for a moment?"

"On one condition," said Damien, handing over his fountain pen, "that you call me *Damien* from now on. I'm not your teacher anymore, and I'd very much like to be your friend."

"Thank you, Damien," she answered shyly. Then on the back of the magazine she had meant to give to Leo, she wrote a message of gratitude for Damien's having taught her to write and to love writing. She then signed her *nom de plume*. "The secret you have to keep is my true identity. Only a few people in the world know that I am really Dusky Nightshade."

"This is too rich!" Damien laughed. "I love it. Thank you from the bottom of my heart. You've made my day."

"Is that your magazine?" Leo asked from the open door to the kitchen.

"I'll have a copy for you tomorrow," Dawn told him. "Or I can go out to the tree house right now and put together another one."

"No, no, please don't leave. Tea's almost ready, and the scones will be coming out any moment."

"May I take a quick peek at what you've been working on lately?" Damien asked Leo.

"Of course, but don't be long."

Dawn followed Damien to the studio, and together they arranged the paintings for viewing. There were but three that Damien had not seen before, and only one that was new to Dawn, a half-finished nude portrait of a young, pretty Asian woman. Damien and Dawn discussed the merits of the various paintings and discovered, to their mutual surprise, that his favorites were also her favorites. Shortly Leo called them to tea.

"Who's the Chinese lady in the painting on the easel?" Dawn asked Leo as he poured her tea.

"She's not Chinese. She's Vietnamese. Her name is *Emmanuelle Long*. She works at the dry-cleaner's shop just over the bridge. I've wanted to paint her since the first time I saw her. But she has very little English. She's hard to talk to. So imagine my delight when she showed up here this morning with Blanca Flores."

"Blanca is Dulce's mother, right?" Dawn guessed.

"That's right. Blanca stopped by to let me know that her fiancé wanted to call on me this afternoon in order to discuss a possible commission." Leo paused to glance at his watch. "Apparently, he really liked the portrait I did of Dulce and wants one of his own daughter. In any case, Emmanuelle is Blanca's next-door neighbor. She was driving Blanca around this morning because Blanca's car is in the shop. When I expressed an interest in having Emmanuelle sit for me, Blanca explained to her in French what I was asking. At first she seemed reluctant, but when she saw my pictures of Blanca, she changed her mind."

Abner Hopewell arrived at 5:00 and was given a tour of Leo's studio and a private exhibition of his paintings. Leo found Abner likable and easy-going. Nor did Abner seem the least bit disconcerted about his future wife's having posed nude for several of the pictures on display. Indeed, as soon as the terms of

87

the commission were agreed upon and a date was set for his daughter's sitting, he selected one of those nude portraits of Blanca and wrote a check for it.

Meanwhile Dawn was showing Damien the tree house. At the little table, he helped her assemble several more copies of the magazine. Then as she autographed one for Leo and another for Mercy, he scribbled out a short poem he had composed in his mind during the collating-and-stapling process.

"What are you writing?" Dawn asked.

"Something to put in your magazine someday if you ever feel like it."

Dawn read what Damien had just penned. "This is terrific. I'll definitely use this. Thanks a lot."

"When you get the rest of these magazines assembled, I can distribute a dozen or so for you."

"Wonderful. How shall I get them to you?"

"Just give them to Leo. He can pass them to me."

# XIII

## JENNIFER

Jennifer Hopewell's sitting was scheduled for Saturday morning. Her step-sister-to-be, Dulce Flores, accompanied her to Leo's apartment, arriving just as Dawn, Starr, and Peggy got there. Leo invited them all in and served them hot cocoa and bran muffins. Neither Peggy nor Starr had ever met Dulce; although they had heard about her from Dawn. Jennifer had only recently been introduced to Dulce for the first time and did not know the others at all.

Getting acquainted was awkward, but Leo allowed the girls as much time as they needed.

Eventually, though, it was time for everyone to get to work. Leo led Jennifer to the studio and posed her on the same kitchen stool Dawn had sat upon for her portrait. Dawn, Starr, and Peggy adjourned to the tree house, leaving Dulce behind to watch Leo work and to chat with Jennifer. However, Dulce quickly grew bored and excused herself to see what was going on in the tree house. Dawn put her to work. Later, when Leo gave Jennifer a break, Dawn gave her crew a break too, and the four went inside to visit with Leo and Jennifer and to take refreshment.

By the end of the day, all five girls had developed a close camaraderie. Dawn was tempted to ask both Jennifer and Dulce, who, incidentally, were almost exactly the same age, to join her tract society. She hesitated only because she was yet unsure what their religious convictions might be. She did give them each a copy of her magazine and swear them to absolute secrecy regarding the true identities of the Little Heathens.

"You can trust us," Jennifer promised. "We won't even tell our closest friends. This will be strictly between us. Right, Dulce?"

"Right," Dulce agreed, "I won't breathe a word to anybody."

Dawn mailed Brenda and Beryl each a dozen copies of the magazine to distribute in any manner they could. Leo consented to keep a stack of them in his studio and to give one to every visitor he had. Of course, Damien and Mercy, each took a little stack as well. Soon all the copies yet assembled were gone. Dawn could only hope that most of them would actually be read. She immediately sat down with Peggy and Starr to plan their second issue.

Then on a Sunday afternoon in May, Brenda quite unexpectedly called on Dawn at home. Her mother, she said, was at Mercy's house and would especially like to meet Dawn.

"May I go?" Dawn begged her mother. "Please, may I go?"

"I don't see why not," Helen said. "Just be home in plenty of time for supper."

Dawn assumed that Carmen would actually be at Leo's apartment, but Carmen was indeed at Mercy's, and so too was Leo. They had not wished to ask Brenda to lie.

Carmen rose and offered Dawn her hand. "So you're the girl genius behind *Dusky Nightshade's Opuscule*. I'm very pleased to meet you."

"I'm glad to meet you too."

"I so approve of what you're doing and so want you to succeed," Carmen told Dawn, "that I've decided to run some ads for your little journal in a few radical periodicals. I think you can pick up quite a few subscribers that way and maybe even get some literary contributions. Of course, if you have any objection, I shan't do it."

"I wouldn't have to pay for it myself?"

"Not a cent."

"Then do it,' Dawn urged. "By all means, do it. And thank you."

"Would you like to help me design the ads?" Carmen offered.

"I shouldn't know how. Might I just watch and learn from you."

"Very well then. Here are the magazines I want to advertise in. I thought you'd like to see them."

Dawn looked through the publications that Carmen had brought. "I've never heard of any of these before. I don't even think the public library has them."

"Probably not," Leo said. "Peggy's father waged a big campaign a few years ago to have all material he deemed objectionable removed from the library. Mercy was the new head librarian then. She resisted his efforts and ended up losing her job."

"No, no," Mercy corrected him. "You make it sound as if I got fired. I didn't; I resigned in protest of decisions made over my head."

"I'm sorry," Dawn said. "I never even knew anything about that. Reverend Wainwright is such a creep. Nobody with any sense likes him."

"And yet your family and Starr's are members of his congregation," Leo reminded her.

"He has them all fooled. They think that he's God's anointed prophet."

At Carmen's suggestion, Dawn sent complimentary copies of *Opuscule* to the American Humanist Association, the American Ethical Union, and a dozen other non-profit organizations committed to rationalism and progressive values.

In early June, Blanca Flores and Abner Hopewell were wed at the Unitarian-Universalist Church in San Antonio, where they had met just a few months earlier. Only their two daughters stood up with them. Mercy and Damien attended the ceremony together. Leo attended with Carmen and her family.

Abner and Jennifer, having let go their apartment in San Antonio, now moved to New Braunfels to live with Blanca and Dulce. The house was small. The two girls would have to share a bedroom, but they did not object in the least. They were, in fact, thrilled to be sisters and eagerly looked forward to attending school together in the fall.

Dulce's longtime best friend next door, Verity Long, soon became Jennifer's best friend as well. The three girls went everywhere together that summer. Blanca called them the *three Graces*.

Of course, Peggy, Starr, and Dawn were also known to some in New Braunfels as the *three Graces*. But this summer, they were joined by a fourth, Leo's granddaughter Brenda, and everyone knows that the Graces are only three.

Now began in earnest work on the second issue of *Opuscule*. Even Beryl was back on the job in Houston. She called Dawn long distance, promised to visit in July, and asked for a new writing assignment to keep her busy until then. She apologized for having been so remiss, but put the blame on the opposite gender. "I'm just no good for anything else when I have boys on my mind. If I had any sense at all, I'd leave them alone completely."

# XIV
## BUFFY

Just before the summer term was to begin at the University of Texas, Robyn Benedict called on Leo to say good-bye and to beg for some of the sketches he had made of her last winter. He was, of course, happy to oblige her, and in return, she promised to sit for another painting when she returned home for the next school holiday.

Accompanying Robyn today was another former model of Leo's, Buffy Mayfield, who had graduated from high school with Robyn a year ago. Last summer she had been Leo's favorite model, but in September, when she had wed, her new husband had put an end to her posing for him. This was the first time Leo had seen her since then. She was pregnant now, though barely showing, and Leo was mad to paint her again.

"Oh, Leo, I don't think so. In my condition, I'm not very attractive. I wouldn't feel comfortable letting anybody see me naked."

"Buffy, you're no less beautiful and no less desirable than the last time you were here."

"That's not what my husband thinks. He tells me all the time how fat and ugly I am."

"Then he's a fool and not a very nice person. Why do you stay with him?"

"Leave her be, Leo," Robyn scolded. "She's got all she can deal with at the moment."

Leo was quick to apologize. "I'm terribly sorry. I had no right—"

"No, no, Robyn, it's okay," Buffy insisted. "Leo makes me feel good about myself, like I haven't felt in a long, long time." Then turning to Leo, she asked, "Do you really think I'd still be a good model?"

"Oh, yes, without a doubt."

Leo suspected that Buffy had hoped all along to be asked to pose for him again and only wanted assurance that the request was sincerely meant. In any case, when Robyn left, Buffy stayed behind. And the painting that resulted was a stunningly sensual celebration of young womanhood. Buffy was as pleased with it as was Leo. And the sexual pleasure they shared at the conclusion of the sitting was the most intense that either of them could remember ever having experienced.

"It's funny too, because I'm not even in love with you," Buffy murmured. "Just imagine how incredible it would have been if we were in love."

Leo was unsure exactly how to respond. "Mmm."

Buffy sat upright on the bed and gazed straight into Leo's face. "You not in love with me, are you? Tell me you're not."

"I'm terribly fond of you, Buffy. But in love? No."

"Good. I'm glad, because being in love is the pits. I used to be so much in love with Bobby I thought I'd die if I couldn't have him. And now I can't stand him. When we first met, everything about him was exciting. He was beautiful to look at and wild and dangerous. I was sure that being married to him would be heaven on earth, and for about a month, I guess, it was. He was sweet and considerate until he started getting bored with me, and when that happened, he quit trying to hide his true nature, which is mean and selfish and disrespectful and violent. Everything turned sour almost overnight. Bobby was sorry he'd married me and didn't want me anymore, but his parents wouldn't let him throw me out. He's very close to them, and they're extremely religious. They don't believe in divorce. But anyway, I left him, went home to my mother, and she wouldn't take me back. She said I had made my bed and now I had to sleep in it. Well, I didn't have anywhere else to go, and I didn't have any money. There was nothing for me to do but go back to Bobby. Now, I'll probably be stuck there for the rest of my life."

Leo had an idea how he might help Buffy out of her bad situation and benefit himself in the bargain. "Do you remember Petra? Was she working here when you used to come for sittings?"

"She was your maid, right?"

"That's right. She used to work two days a week, all day Tuesday and half a day on Saturday. I only paid her minimum wage for twelve hours a week, but she had other part-time employers too; so she managed to get by. However, she's not with me anymore. Would you consider a job like that beneath you?"

"No, not at all. Why should I mind getting paid to do what I do at home for free? But, Leo, Bobby would just take all my money. I'd never save enough to be able to move out."

"What I have in mind is a live-in arrangement." Leo rolled out of bed and put on his robe. "Come. Let me show you the spare bedroom."

Without bothering to cover her nudity, Buffy followed Leo down the hall to his guest room. It was large and airy, she noted, though not so large as Leo's own bedroom. Windows overlooked the street in front and the driveway on the west side. More significantly, an outside door to the front porch would allow her to come and go without having to pass through the living room or the studio. It was such a perfect solution to her problem that she felt an almost irresistible urge to cry.

"I can't pay you any more than I was paying Petra," Leo told her. "But room and board should be worth something, don't you think?"

"Oh, absolutely. This is ideal, almost too good to be true. Are you sure you're willing to do this?"

"Are you kidding? To have my number-one model in residence, what could be better for me? There is one point we need to settle, however. Your job title will be *housekeeper*, not *maid*. You will not be a mere servant. You will be in charge of running this household, and if ever I begin to sell enough paintings, I'll raise your salary to reflect that fact."

"Don't worry. I'll keep this whole place spotless, and I'm even a pretty fair cook. You'll never be sorry you hired me."

As previously agreed, Robyn returned when called by Buffy to collect her and take her home. The following morning, as soon as Bobby had left for work, Buffy loaded all her personal possessions into her own vehicle, a beat-up but dependable old Bronco; then leaving Bobby a terse note, she closed that chapter of her life.

# XV
## VERITY

Since Memorial Day the population of New Braunfels had multiplied several-fold with tourists pouring in daily, eager to enjoy the water parks, to float down the lazy Comal River on inner tubes, or to raft the white-water rapids of the Guadalupe. Until Labor Day this usually sedate community would remain in party mode. Traffic was now bumper to bumper downtown; sidewalks were crowded with vacationers in swim attire.

Amongst them today were Dawn, Starr, Peggy, and Brenda. With beach towels, inner tubes, and one huge picnic basket, they were on their way to Landa Park to spend the entire day. It was 9:00 in the morning, and they were not expected home until 6:30 in the evening.

Dawn's favorite picnic spot was a uniquely secluded area, where there were but two tables. This morning both tables were vacant. So the girls staked out one, left their basket and towels there, then carrying their inner tubes with them, went for a frolic in the icy-cold shallows of the upper Comal.

Upon their return to their table, they found a party of seven just arriving at the other table. At first Dawn barely glanced their way, but then she thought she heard familiar voices.

"It's Dulce and Jennifer," Peggy whispered. "Shouldn't we go over and say hi to them?"

In fact, that second party consisted of Abner and Blanca, their two daughters, and their next-door neighbors, the Longs. Dawn recognized both Blanca and Emmanuelle from the paintings of them that Leo had done. Verity Long, age ten, was a miniature version of her mother. Mr Long's given name was *Duane*, and his English, while not perfect, was considerably better than his wife's. Dawn warmed to him immediately, and contrived to sit next to him when Blanca and Emmanuelle put out coffee cake and hot cocoa for everyone.

After breakfast Dulce was anxious to show Jennifer a place in the nearby wood where a rope hung from a tree limb extending over the river. "You can swing on it and drop down into the water. It's more fun than sex."

"Now, how would you know that?" Blanca demanded.

"Mama!" Dulce exclaimed. "It's just an expression. Everybody says it."

"It really is fun," Starr agreed. "We used to do that last year, but now the path is overgrown with poison ivy. We won't be able to get there."

"I know a way," Verity piped up. "We can float down the river on our inner tubes. Then we don't have to go through the wood."

Dawn was not convinced. "Won't poison ivy be on the bank where we have to get out?"

"It wasn't last week," Verity claimed.

Jennifer was concerned that with the trail impassable, they might have difficulty getting back. "We can't float upriver, can we?"

"No," said Dulce, "but we can float further down and get out at Prince Solms Park, then walk back by the road."

Jennifer looked at Dawn and Starr for confirmation. "Is that possible?"

"Sure," Dawn said. "It's a long walk, but there's nothing difficult about it."

"The worst part is crossing streets," Verity told them, "because the pavement'll be as hot as a griddle. Luckily, we can keep to the grassy verge most of the way."

"I'm keeping my sneakers on," Starr announced. "You guys should too."

Abner insisted upon some adult's accompanying the girls to that isolated section of the river. Dawn immediately suggested that their chaperone should be Duane. But Duane deferred to Blanca, who was known to be a strong swimmer and had recently completed a course in water safety and lifesaving.

They drifted not in one big cluster, but strung out over a distance of about a hundred feet. Dawn and Jennifer, both natural leaders, took the vanguard. Next came Starr and Dulce, then the three youngest, Peggy, Verity, and Brenda. Blanca brought up the rear, from which position she could keep an eye on all her charges at once.

100

"Daddy was reading your little magazine the other night," Jennifer confided to Dawn. "I think he liked it, because he asked me where I got it."

Dawn was immediately alarmed. "What'd you tell him?"

"Relax. I didn't give away your secret. All I said was that I picked it up at Leo's studio and that Leo had let me keep it."

Dawn breathed a sigh of relief. "I wish we didn't have to be so careful, but honestly, you don't have any idea how much trouble I'd be in if I got caught. Peggy too, and maybe even Starr, though I kind of doubt it. Her mother's really cool."

"It is hard for me to believe," Jennifer admitted. "But I can still respect your wishes. You know, I finally got around to reading most of your magazine myself, and I don't disagree with any of it. Nobody in my family would."

"That's good, because I wanted to ask you and Dulce to join us. I was just afraid you might not approve of what we were doing."

"The Little Heathens' Underground Tract Society and Free Press, you mean?"

"We could really use two extra writers. What do you say?"

"It sounds like a lot of work. I hate having to write essays for school, but maybe this would be different. Let me think about it. And naturally, I'll have to talk it over with Dulce. We'll let you know."

"We're coming to the railroad trestle," Verity shouted. "After that it won't be long. Watch the left bank. It's easy to miss, unless other people are already there."

"I hope we have it to ourselves," Dawn said to Jennifer.

A few minutes later Jennifer spotted a rope dangling from the treetops overhanging the river. "There it is. I see it."

"And there's no one else around," Dawn noted with satisfaction.

All six of the girls climbed out onto the muddy bank and stacked their inner tubes as far from the encroaching poison ivy as possible. Immediately they were attacked by swarms of mosquitoes.

"Oh, oh, oh!" complained Starr. "I'm being eaten alive."

Dulce struck a heroic pose. "Damn the mosquitoes! Full speed ahead."

Dawn climbed the tree to retrieve the rope. "Who wants to go first?"

"Me, me," Starr insisted. "I've got to get back in the water or I'm going to die."

Blanca had remained on her inner tube on the water near the far bank. So as not to float on downstream, she clung to a trailing willow frond.

Starr landed with a huge splash, and when she surfaced, she called to Peggy to throw her an inner tube. Then she paddled out to where Blanca was. She clearly had no intention of getting out onto the bank again and facing the mosquitoes.

Verity swung next, then Brenda, and after Brenda, Peggy. That left only Dulce, Jennifer, and Dawn. Already Verity was scrambling back onto the bank with Brenda right behind her. Dawn handed the rope to Jennifer, who hesitated for so long that Dawn realized she must be terrified of launching herself into space.

Dulce slapped her own face, then her thigh, and finally her arm. "Mosquitoes are an abomination, but they're all the proof I need to know that there's no God."

Dawn bit her lower lip and considered carefully how to respond. "I can't agree. Sorry. Mosquitoes don't prove that there's not a God, only that there's not an all-powerful and benevolent God."

Dulce laughed. "You're absolutely right. I concede."

Still holding the rope and still poised to jump, Jennifer quoted something she had often heard her father say. "'If God is God, He is not good. If God is good, He is not God.'"

"Exactly," said Dawn. "Did you just make that up?"

"Nope. It's by Archibald MacLeish, whoever that is."

Dulce placed both her hands on Jennifer's behind. "Hold on tight, sis." And so saying, she shoved with all her might. Jennifer, shrieking loudly, sailed out over the river and dropped down into the water.

"You're next," Dawn told Dulce. "I'll be right behind you."

As Dulce reached for the rope, there could be heard a crashing in the brush nearby. "Sounds like an elephant coming down the trail."

In the next moment, Junior Weeks emerged from the dense brush and poison ivy, his crew of miscreants close behind him. Dawn had never met Junior, but she understood immediately that he was trouble. The look in his eyes told her all she needed to know about him.

Blanca too grasped the seriousness of the threat. Unfortunately, she was about thirty feet away. She slipped from her inner tube and pushed it toward Starr to keep, then struck out swimming toward the shore.

"We should go," Dulce whispered to Dawn.

"I know," Dawn answered under her breath. "Get everybody into the water and on a tube. I'll be along in a minute."

"I believe I've died and gone to Heaven," Junior exclaimed dramatically. "Girls everywhere and not an ugly one in the bunch. What's your name, cutie?"

Dawn turned to face Junior. "We're just leaving. You guys can have this place, but I've got to warn you, the mosquitoes are terrible here."

"Don't be in such a rush." Junior seized Dawn by the upper arm and swung her around into the clutches of his first lieutenant. "Here you go, Billy. Help this girl scratch her mosquito bites. She won't tell me her name, but maybe she'll tell you."

Dulce was hurrying to get Verity and Brenda back into the water and to push all the inner tubes off the bank. When she felt Junior's hand groping her bottom, she whirled around and tried to slap him, but he caught her wrist and held her fast. Verity and Brenda were just as easily captured by Rodney and Shorty.

Peggy was having none of it. Furious, she climbed out of the water and strode up to Junior and poked him roughly in the chest with her forefinger. "Enough! We found this place first. You'd better get out of here right now."

Junior was momentarily unnerved. "KJV, I didn't see you."

"Well, you see me now, and I warned you what would happen if you ever bothered me again." Then in a monumental bluff, Peggy turned her head to shout up the trail in the opposite direction whence Junior and his gang had come. "Toby! Toby! Come quick!"

The bluff worked. Junior loosed Dawn and fled in panic. His three henchmen immediately followed his example.

Blanca was just climbing out of the water and was amazed to see the four boys fleeing. "What did I miss? What happened?"

Peggy shrugged self-deprecatingly. "I told them I knew karate."

Everyone laughed.

Back at the picnic tables, Blanca used her cell phone to call the Sheriff's Department. Peggy and Starr had been able to furnish her the names of all the marauders, whom deputies later arrested at their homes. Apparently, Dulce's word was all that was needed, for none of the girls was ever to be interviewed by officers. And while none of them would ever learn the exact disposition of the case, neither would any of them ever again be bothered by Junior or his ruffian friends.

# XVI
## TOURIST SEASON

B uffy, in her new rôle as Leo's housekeeper, was always extremely conscientious not to crowd him or intrude upon his personal life. She was almost totally dependent upon him now, and as the days passed, she became increasingly attached to him. She still would have denied being in love with him, but she certainly cared for him and experienced her greatest joy whenever he showed her any small evidence that he cared for her. Feeling more useful here and more appreciated than she had ever before felt, Buffy set about to make herself indispensable. She even chauffeured Leo about and ran errands for him in her own vehicle, which he, in gratitude, insured, maintained, and kept fully fueled.

Her worst fear was that Leo might ever begin to resent her for "cramping his style." When he had female company, she made herself as scarce as possible.  And even though she occasionally felt a slight twinge of jealousy when he took one of his other models into his bedroom, she refused to let that jealousy get the better of her.

To supplement the meager pay she received from Leo, she worked two days a week cleaning house for Mercy. Then too she took in ironing and did hemming and darning. She was always on the lookout for ways to make a little extra money from home. And ninety cents of every dollar she earned went into a savings account.

Buffy was well liked by Dawn, who remembered her from the year before, when Buffy had worked weekdays after school and all day Saturdays at the drug-store soda fountain. No less fond of Buffy was Brenda, who often elected to sleep with her rather than with her grandfather.

Whilst New Braunfels teemed with tourists, Leo had little trouble finding new models every week. Consequently, he tended, during the summer months, to neglect his usual favorites, except for one. Buffy he painted at least once every fortnight, for her body was constantly changing.  Captivated, he meant to portray her at every stage of her pregnancy.

She posed for him (usually in the nude) sitting, standing, and recumbent.  He recorded her every aspect and her every mood.  For Leo, painting had always been an act of worship.  For Buffy, having her entire physical self exposed and under such close scrutiny for hours at a time—being adored and celebrated—constituted the most exquisite foreplay imaginable.  By the end of every sitting, both artist and model would find themselves in the highest possible state of erotic arousal.  Curiously, it was only upon these occasions of artistic collaboration that the two of them were ever sexually intimate with each other.  Their relationship otherwise was defined by casual friendship and mutually respectful accommodation.  Indeed, any observer who did not already know better might easily have assumed that they were brother and sister, or more likely, father and daughter.

Besides Buffy, Leo these days rarely employed any one model more than once.  During the early spring, he had often painted the little girls who frequented the tree house and visited his studio, and he intended in the fall to resume that practice, but for now he simply had not time to paint them.  On any day that Leo had no one lined up to pose for him, he would take an easel to Prince Solms Park and begin a landscape with picnickers and bathers, inevitably attracting an enchanted audience, amongst whom would be at least one lovely young woman with an irresistible desire to be immortalized on canvas.

Two or three times a week, Brenda and Dawn helped Leo carry his painting supplies to the park, for which assistance he kept them in spending money.  They were thus able to enjoy milkshakes, onion rings, hamburgers, or pizza whenever they felt like it.

On a sweltering day in mid-June, having worked in the tree house all morning on the layout of Issue Number Two of *Opuscule*, Dawn and Brenda decided to treat themselves to lunch at the drugstore soda fountain downtown.  In the studio Leo was working on a nude portrait of a college sophomore from a small town in Oklahoma, a girl named *Trish*. When Brenda stuck her head in the door to tell Leo that she and Dawn were leaving, Trish seemed to blush all over.

Brenda smiled to herself and tried to imagine how she would feel standing there completely bare and having someone pop in unexpectedly. "I'd probably blush too," she told Dawn.

Brenda's notion of the ideal lunch was likewise Dawn's: pimento-cheese sandwich on toast, dill pickles and potato chips on the side, tomato soup with oyster crackers, and root beer in a frosted mug. Dawn and Brenda also agreed that this particular soda fountain was probably the best place in the whole world to get just such a lunch.

As their dirty dishes were being cleared away and they were discussing whether or not to order dessert, they were unexpectedly joined by Jennifer and Dulce.

"Hey!" said Dawn. "What are you guys doing here?"

"Shopping for a birthday present," Dulce answered. "Mama's going to be twenty-one next Sunday."

Jennifer felt the need to clarify that claim. "Actually, it's more like thirty-one, but she tells everybody twenty-one. It's sort of a joke."

"We have something for you, by the way," Dulce informed Dawn, "not with us, but at the house. We were going to take it to Leo's tomorrow, but if you'd like to come home with us, you can have it today."

Dawn glanced at Brenda to see whether she had any objection. "Sure, we can do that. Where do you live?"

"It's pretty far, but we're on our bikes. What about you?"

"We're afoot."

"No problem. We can double up. We do it all the time with Verity. Then when you're ready to leave, you can borrow one of our bikes. We'll pick it up at Leo's tomorrow."

"Is it a surprise, what you have for me?" Dawn asked. "Or can you tell me what it is?"

"Don't get too excited," Jennifer cautioned. "It's only some articles for your magazine."

"Even Verity wrote one," Dulce added.

"You weren't supposed to discuss this with anybody but Dulce," Dawn reminded Jennifer.

"We didn't tell her the secret part," Jennifer swore. "She doesn't even know it's you she's working for. She just saw what we were doing and wanted to do the same. So we gave her an assignment, and she completed it."

"We did show her the magazine," Dulce admitted, "but we didn't tell her that you're Dusky Nightshade."

Dawn was still concerned. "What will her parents say? Aren't they Christians? Her mother wears a cross on a chain around her neck."

"A crucifix actually," said Jennifer. "Emmanuelle is a Catholic, and Verity goes to a Catholic school. But Duane is a Buddhist. So you see, nobody in that house can afford to be too fanatical. They have to be pretty tolerant just to get along together."

Dawn was pleasantly surprised to discover on the living-room coffee table in the Flores-Hopewell home copies of the same radical magazines that Carmen had run advertisements in. If Abner and Blanca were subscribers, then surely they too were on the side of enlightenment and should be made privy to her most-sensitive secrets. Every new ally she made improved her chances of making a difference in the world.

In keeping with the tradition established by Dawn herself, Jennifer, Dulce, and Verity had all assumed false identities. Jennifer's was *Hope Wells*; Dulce's was *Candy Flowers*; and Verity's was *Misty Du*.

"Du," Jennifer explained, "was Duane's original surname when he lived in Vietnam, his whole name being *Du Te Long*. But here surnames come last; so he changed his name to *Duane Long*. If he had simply reversed the order to *Long Du*, as he might have done, Verity's real last name would then have been *Du*."

Dawn scratched her head. "That's all very confusing. But if you want to tell your parents everything about the Little Heathens and you think we can trust them, then it's okay with me. The Longs too, I suppose. But only if they absolutely swear a sacred oath never to reveal anything that could get Peggy and me into trouble."

On the first day of summer, Beryl arrived in New Braunfels just in time to help Dawn and Brenda collate and staple the new issue of *Opuscule*. With Peggy temporarily grounded for some minor infraction at home and Starr on vacation in Canada with her mother, the Little Heathens were frightfully short-handed. Even Jennifer, Dulce, and Verity were away for a few days, their two families having rented a beach house together at Padre Island. It seemed like forever before all the magazines were assembled.

Relieved to have that daunting chore behind them, the three girls climbed Leo's back stairs in search of refection.  In the studio Leo was working on a double nude portrait of freckle-faced blonde sisters from Little Rock, Arkansas.  Neither Brenda nor Dawn had any particular desire to hang around and watch, but Beryl, who had never before had the opportunity to observe an artist at work was enthralled.  Insomuch as his two models did not seem to mind, Leo gave her permission to stay.

Dawn and Brenda were as much at home in Leo's kitchen as in their own.  They found Hot Pockets in the freezer and popped them into the microwave oven, then opened sodas and poured them over ice.  When their food was hot, Dawn took Beryl's out to her before sitting down with Brenda in the breakfast room.  Later, as they were washing their plates at the sink, Buffy returned from shopping and enlisted the aid of all three girls to help her carry in the groceries and put them away.

"How's the painting coming?" Buffy asked Beryl.

"It must be almost done.  I heard Leo tell Sandy and Amanda they wouldn't need another break, because they'd be through before it would be time for one."

Buffy suggested a plan to get the girls out of the house.  "I've been thinking of something fun for us to do for the rest of the afternoon.  How would you three like to visit the Schlitterbahn?"

Beryl and Brenda were eager to leave immediately, but Dawn felt that they should wait for Leo to get finished, so he could accompany them.

Buffy speculated that a trip to the water park was the last thing on Leo's mind at the moment.

"Let's just make this an all-girl expedition. You and Beryl run home and get your bathing suits on."

"Are you going to go down the slide too?" Brenda asked doubtfully.

"No, no," Buffy laughed. "I don't think the baby would like such vigorous activity. Anyway, I couldn't begin to wiggle into a bathing suit. But I'll enjoy watching you guys. Now, chop-chop, let's get moving."

At home Dawn put on her bathing suit under her clothes, then dashed back to Leo's apartment. Buffy and the other two girls were waiting for her inside the car in the driveway. They had a pleasant excursion, each of the girls going down the winding water slide several times. Beryl even managed to meet and flirt with a couple of boys. And upon their return, they found Leo in the kitchen, preparing supper. The painting on the easel was complete; the models for it were long gone. It was now after 6:00. So Dawn and Beryl bade the others a good-night and hurried home to their own suppers.

# XVII
## Fourth of July

At the urging of both Mercy and Buffy, Leo consented to hold a studio open house to coincide with Mercy's annual backyard barbecue in July. Most of the hundred or so guests would be members of the Griffoun Society in Austin. Also invited would be Leo's daughter and her family from San Antonio and all Leo's local models and their families.

The date was set for the second Saturday in the month. Mercy's caterer would arrive at mid-day and set up an old-time chuck wagon in the driveway. Guests should begin arriving in the early afternoon. To avoid having to invite Dawn's parents, who would certainly have taken umbrage at Leo's nude paintings, Mercy represented the affair as a club function and begged Helen's permission to hire Dawn and her two best girlfriends to serve beverages.

"Do you mean alcoholic beverages?"

"Oh, no," Mercy assured her. "The Griffoun Society is strictly no alcohol, no tobacco, no drugs. That's what we're all about. There'll be iced tea, lemonade, and soft drinks. Beryl and Brenda will both be helping out, but I need three more. I can pay them fifty dollars each."

Dawn, standing at her mother's side, was so astonished at the prospect of such generous remuneration that she swallowed her gum.

"Will they be late?" Helen wanted to know.

"Late but hopefully not too late. The serving is pretty light duty, more fun than work. When I really need them is after everyone else is gone to help me clean up."

Helen considered carefully. "Alright, but I'd like to have them in by midnight if at all possible. I'll speak to the other girls' mothers and arrange everything."

On the day of the party, Dawn, Starr, and Peggy wore similar white sundresses with spaghetti straps and on their feet white sandals. As they arrived, a mariachi band was just warming up.

"What do we have to do first?" Starr asked Mercy.

"All you have to do today is have fun. That business about hiring you to serve was just a ruse to get you here, and the fifty dollars I'm going to pay you when I take you home tonight is, in fact, a literary grant. I want you to think of it that way."

None of the three had ever before heard of a literary grant, but they thanked Mercy nonetheless, then went in search of Beryl, whom they soon spotted in conversation with Robyn Benedict and another young woman of college age. Before introductions could be made, Robyn excused herself to go meet Damien, who was just arriving.

The second young woman, Robyn's new roommate Bootsy, herself an aspiring writer, was particularly interested in the Little Heathens' literary activities. As a teenager, she had managed to get a single short story published. Serious essays of opinion, however, had never been her thing. She had only ever written one such that she could recall and that one at the age of thirteen. "I'll send it to you. If you can use it in your *Opuscule*, you're more than welcome to it. Just make sure your readers know I wrote it when I was much younger."

By mid-afternoon, scores of guests had arrived and were clustered about the front, back, and side yards in the shade of trees and under beach umbrellas.  Inside the studio Leo was showing his paintings and discussing art with whomever Mercy and Buffy could steer his way.

Brenda, who had gone home to San Antonio only a week ago, returned today with her parents, arriving just minutes before Jennifer, Dulce, and Verity showed up with their parents.  Never before had all eight members of the tract society been together in one place.  Dawn was eager to have a group photograph made of them, and Carmen was happy to oblige. She borrowed Mercy's camera to take the picture.

The only other minors present were a boy of about fifteen years and twin girls, age four.  The boy soon gravitated to Beryl, or perhaps she gravitated to him.  In any case, the two of them spent a lot of time alone together in the tree house that day.

The buffet would not open until late.  In the meantime there were mountains of canapés.  Cold beverages included all that Mercy had mentioned to Helen, plus alcohol-free wine and Near Beer.

Dawn, Starr, and Peggy thought it best to stick to lemonade, but Dulce and Jennifer both drank Near Beer, and the other three Little Heathens were seen with wine glasses in their hands.

When Dawn went inside once to use the bathroom, she heard muffled voices from behind Buffy's bedroom door.  Curious, she tip-toed closer, not to eavesdrop exactly, but only to find out who was in there that possibly should not be.

"I don't care whether you had sex with him before or not."  It was Buffy's voice.  But to whom was she speaking? And about whom?  "It's just that if you did it the other times, you'd better do it next time too if you want us to still be friends.  I can't have him thinking you're acting differently because of me."

116

Someone answered, but Dawn could not identify the voice or understand the words. Ashamed of herself for having overheard as much as she already had, she quickly entered the hall bathroom and locked the door behind her. However, some oddity of the acoustics in this old house only served to amplify the conversation in the next room.

"I don't know if I should tell you this or not, but Bobby's been coming up to Austin to see me." The voice could now be clearly identified as Robyn's.

"My Bobby?"

"I went out with him in high school a few times before he started going steady with you. Now he wants to get back together with me."

"Well, you're welcome to him."

"Don't get huffy with me. After the way he treated you, I'm not the least bit interested in him, but he won't take any discouragement. So it occurred to me the other night that maybe I could do you a favor by getting him to file for divorce. I told him that I'd never go out with a married man, because it was against my principles. But I sort of hinted that if he were legally free, I might be more interested."

"That won't work," Buffy asserted. "He'll never go against his parents, and they're totally opposed to divorce."

"Girl, you underestimate pussy power. You'd better be thinking what you want out of this divorce, because you can dictate the terms  While Bobby thinks he has a chance of getting into my pants, which, by the way, he never did in high school, all you have to do is threaten to withhold his freedom. Tell him you you've changed your mind and you want a reconciliation. He'll offer you the moon just to get you to sign the papers."

"But I don't want anything from him. I wish I didn't ever have to see him again."

"You're entitled to child support," Robyn reminded her.

"I don't need it, and I don't want him to have anything to do with me or my child. Let me tell you something. When he first found out he was going to be a father, he was pretty excited, because he wanted a son. But after the amniocentesis, when we found out it was a girl, he lost all interest. In fact, he started saying that she probably wasn't even his."

"Then maybe I could convince him that there really is a possibility that she's somebody else's. Of course, I don't dare be too convincing, because if he asks for DNA testing to prove that he's not the father, it would only prove that he is. Right?"

"I'm afraid so. But I'll let him off without child support if he'll just agree to stay out of our lives and leave us alone. In fact, I'd be happy to swear to his parents that my baby is not really their grandchild. He might go for that."

When the chuck-wagon cook finally rang the chow bell for people to start queuing up, Mercy sought out Dawn and tried to hand her a large basket to deliver to her family. In it were covered dishes of barbecued pork and smoked sausages, potato salad, coleslaw, deviled eggs, pickles and jalapeños, baked beans, and buttermilk biscuits. The basket, however, was too heavy for Dawn to lift. So Mercy offered to carry it if Dawn would accompany her.

"I hope we're back before they quit serving," Dawn said.

"Don't worry. The buffet'll be open for a while yet. You'll have plenty of time to eat."

As they walked the few blocks to the Ramsey home, Dawn asked Mercy if she were terribly rich. "I mean, because you don't even have a job, and this party must be costing you a fortune. That's what Mom said this morning."

"I inherited a little bit of money from my grandmother, also the house, and I've invested carefully. I can live pretty much as I please, but I'm not rich, not like the Rockefellers or Bill Gates. By the way, speaking of fat cats, did you meet Simon Estes?"

"I think so. I've met so many people today I forget their names."

"Simon never comes to my parties. He always says it's too far to drive. But I knew that he was intrigued by what you and the other girls were doing; so I promised him you'd be here. Apparently, that did the trick."

"Is he the white-haired old man in a suit and tie?"

"That's Simon, always overdressed. He owns one of the bookstores that handle your literature, the one in Austin."

"He wanted me to come up to Austin in September and read a few of my essays aloud at some kind of dinner program."

Mercy was astonished. "Not the Griffoun Society's Annual Black-Tie Banquet?"

"Yeah, I think that's what he said. Of course, there's no way I can go, but I thanked him for inviting me."

Mercy laughed. "You have no idea what an honor he has conferred upon you. The Griffoun Society has had Lawrence Casler, Isaac Asimov, Robert Rimmer, Christopher Hitchens, and scads of other famous writers to address their annual banquet."

"Gee! I didn't know that. But I still can't go."

Later, as twilight descended, Japanese lanterns were lit in the backyard, where a small temporary dance floor had been constructed. The band switched to softer music, and several couples got up to dance. Dawn was asked first by Damien, who patiently taught her a simple box step, and then by Leo. When, after several numbers, Duane had still not asked her, she summoned the courage to ask him. He accepted, but he did not, as she had fantasized, utter words of endearment in her ear as they danced or even try to flirt with her. Simply by being so respectfully formal, he managed to communicate to her that he did not reciprocate her feelings toward him. In her disappointment, it seemed as if the song would never end. She was saved from utter humiliation only by the graciousness of Duane's expression of gratitude for the great honor of dancing with her.

Leo and Damien each seemed intent on dancing with every female present. When Buffy had had her turn with each of them, she sat down with Dawn on the back stairs to watch the goings on. The crowd was thinning out. Perhaps half the guests had gone home, but those that remained showed no sign that they were anywhere near ready to stop partying. There were even a few same-gender couples dancing now.

"Lots of ladies are dancing together," Dawn observed. "So I guess it's okay. Would you like to dance with me?"

Buffy smiled brightly. "I'd love to."

Buffy and Dawn did not dance well together. Dawn was still a novice dancer, and Buffy was unused to leading. But they enjoyed themselves immensely.

"I hope people don't think we're lesbians," Dawn whispered.

"Let them think what they want.  I don't give a rat's ass.  I'm having more fun than I've had all evening."

"When's your baby due?"

"Not till October.  I can't wait."

"Be glad you're not an elephant.  You'd have to be pregnant for almost two years."

"Oh, God!  What a thought!"  Buffy giggled.  "I guess that's something to be thankful for."

"What if she's born on Halloween?  Trick or treat?"

Buffy laughed aloud.  "I like your sense of humor. You don't seem like a little kid at all."

"I'm not," Dawn quipped.  "I'm a twenty-year-old midget."

# XVIII
## AUTUMN

The remainder of the summer flew by so swiftly that Dawn could hardly believe her ears when her mother announced that it was time to shop for school. On the last Saturday before the beginning of the new school year, Helen Ramsey drove Dawn and Meghan down to San Antonio to buy them new coats and shoes, play clothes, Sunday dresses, and school uniforms Dawn would also be getting her first brassiere. She did not want one, did not really need one for support, and could not begin to appreciate her mother's concern for her modesty. This same issue had arisen last year, and Dawn had prevailed. This year her mother stood firm.

When their shopping was complete, they stopped for lunch at an outdoor café near the uniform shop they had just come from. As they were ordering, Carmen and Brenda happened to sit down at the table next to theirs. Dawn had not seen Brenda for a month, and to tell the truth, she had been so busy that she had scarcely thought about her. On their last parting, the two girls had promised to exchange letters, but neither had taken the initiative to write first. Today, the moment they recognized each other, they jumped to their feet and embraced as long-lost sisters. Dawn then made proper introductions, first presenting Carmen to Helen, then Meghan to Carmen.

"This elder daughter of yours has the best manners of any child I've ever known," Carmen remarked to Helen.

"I have often said the same of your daughter. We two must be outstanding mothers."

"What about me?" Meghan piped up. "I have good manners too."

Carmen laughed and ruffled Meghan's hair. "You are an absolute angel. Where did you get all that curly, blonde hair?"

"I didn't get it anywhere," Meghan defended herself. "It's mine."

"Why don't you two move over here to our table?" Helen suggested.

The two women enjoyed a pleasant conversation over lunch, than lingered for coffee and dessert. Dawn and Brenda could say very little of significance without giving away secrets. Still, Dawn did manage to whisper in Brenda's ear that if she intended to be represented in Issue Number Three of *Opuscule*, she should get a new essay in the post soon.

Response to Carmen's ads had so far netted about twenty subscriptions, all out of state, one literary contribution from a teenage boy in Waxahachie, and three letters from journalists curious about the tract society itself. Dawn had answered all the letters in long hand, enclosing with each reply one free copy of her *Opuscule*.

On the day after Mercy's barbecue, when Damien had first learned of Simon's impossible request to have Dawn address the Griffoun Society and two hundred paying guests, he had suggested an alternative. Why not allow Dawn to send as her surrogate some other member of her group? Starr and Peggy were obviously out of the question, and Beryl probably lived too far away. But surely any of the other four might attend in Dawn's place. There had ensued a great deal of discussion and negotiation, but in the end, it had been decided that Verity, Dulce, and Jennifer would all three go and that the very sizable speaker's fee would go into the Little Heathens' general treasury.

While Dawn was extremely disappointed not to be going herself, she was nonetheless thankful for Damien's suggestion. She was rushing now to get the new issue out before the big night. Her hope was that every person attending would accept a free copy. That would mean producing twice as many as last time, four times as many as the first time. Henceforth, she would be printing, collating, and stapling at Kinko's.

Labor Day came and went. New Braunfels suddenly seemed a ghost town. It might take days or even weeks before the uncrowded streets felt normal again.

With the little girls in school and the mobs of tourists gone, Leo asked Buffy to drive him out River Road in search of dramatic scenery to paint. He had no difficulty finding the perfect spot. He set his easel up beneath some cypress trees beside the Guadalupe River. Buffy stayed only a little while to chat with him, then left him there alone and drove back into town to do laundry. She would pick him up later in the day.

At noon Leo ate the picnic lunch he had brought, and completed the painting by 2:00. After that he went walking along the water's edge enjoying his solitude. It occurred to him to try to locate the Wynter Palace, Damien's pretentiously named riverfront cabin, the address of which was Hueco

Falls. But in truth, Leo had no idea whether he was above that location or below it.

In all the hours he was out there on the river, no more than six vehicles passed on the nearby roadway, and he saw neither boater nor fisherman on the water. It was such a pleasant day and he was so satisfied with the painting he produced that he decided to repeat this outing at least once a week throughout the fall.

Buffy encouraged Leo to enter a painting in the upcoming juried art show associated with Wurstfest, the New Braunfels version of Oktoberfest. He had not done so last year, but to please Buffy, he agreed. It would be unwise in such a small town, he felt, to enter a nude, but he had a number of other works to choose from. It would have to be a small picture, however, because the purchase prize was so meager.

"Other art fairs are coming up around the state," Buffy informed him. "You should let me set up a booth and sell your paintings directly to the public."

"You seem to forget, Buffy, that you're going to have your hands full taking care of this baby."

"You're right, I know. It's just that I do so want to help. You're a wonderful artist, Leo. But nobody is going to buy your pictures if they never get a chance to see them?"

"Have you ever been to any of those art fairs? Do people actually buy paintings there?"

"I used to go all the time. There are huge crowds, and everybody buys something. It could be just a little inexpensive craft item, or it could be an enormous painting. And remember, lots of the people who go there would never set foot inside an art gallery. So even if you someday get the best galleries in the world to handle your work, you'll still be missing out if you don't do the art fairs and swap meets too."

Fully one third of Leo's body of work to date consisted of images of Buffy. Nor were all these images nudes. He had painted her ironing, cleaning house, cooking, reading, sleeping, and combing her hair. Images of Dawn constituted his second largest portfolio, but of course, he could not show those. Between terms, he had painted Robyn again, and in Austin for some club function, he had run into Bootsy, and she too had consented to pose for him. But she could hardly be expected to come all the way to New Braunfels for a sitting; and so it was incumbent on him to arrange the use of a studio in Austin. This challenge he was currently working on.

Meanwhile Dawn visited Leo each weekday after school, as she had last spring, and on Saturdays whenever possible. She watched him paint and chatted with his models. She read his books, especially the little handmade journal, *Observations and Contemplations*, which was often a source of new ideas for her and the Little Heathens to write about. She helped Buffy with her chores, and indeed, she felt that here was where she belonged, much more so than in her parents' home.

Buffy's belly was getting bigger by the day. Surely it could not be long now until she delivered.

"Your tummy's as big as a watermelon," Dawn informed her one day in the studio, "and as tight as a drum. It's amazing! I don't see how one little baby could make you that big."

Buffy was once more posing nude for Leo. "You think it might be twins?"

"More like a whole litter, I'd say."

126

Buffy laughed so hard that Leo had to re-position her head, arms, and knees after she had regained her composure.

"Leo," Buffy said, "do you think I could adopt this girl to be my little sister? She's more fun to be around than anybody I know."

Leo smiled benevolently. "Everybody wants to adopt Dawn. I'd like to myself."

"Oh, oh! Come quick," Buffy urged. "The baby's kicking."

Dawn and Leo put their hands on Buffy's abdomen.

"Can you feel it?" Buffy asked. "Oh, there it goes again."

Suddenly Dawn assumed the persona of her favorite Star Trek character. "Captain, our sensors are picking up an alien life form. I recommend we send in a probe."

"No fucking way!" Buffy objected. "A goddamned probe is how this episode began."

Leo, Dawn, and Buffy all broke up laughing and had difficulty stopping.

"I shouldn't laugh this much," Buffy managed to say. "This baby has her knees against my bladder. I'm afraid I'll pee on the chair."

Of course, that brought on even more laughter. When at length the frivolity subsided, Leo very patiently helped Buffy recover her pose.

Thirty minutes later, Leo announced completion of the picture, and Buffy whispered to Dawn, "I have a private matter to discuss with Leo. Would you mind excusing us?"

The following afternoon Buffy invited Dawn to go shopping with her. "I need to buy baby things. You can help me pick them out. Afterward we can stop at the drug store for ice-cream sodas. What do you say?"

Dawn could hardly believe that Buffy was still in need of anything for the nursery. In August Robyn had organized a huge shower, inviting all their girlfriends from high school. And shortly thereafter, Mercy had paid for a complete set of nursery furniture to be picked out by Buffy herself. That had been delivered a week ago. There were mountains of diapers and more than one diaper pail. There were bottles and blankets and boodles of baby clothes, not to mention a stroller, a car seat, a baby carrier, and a really classy pram, this last item being a gift from Leo. Still, a shopping expedition with a grown-up friend promised to be an exciting adventure. Dawn did not hesitate to say yes.

They went first to a department store, then made stops at a maternity shop, a toy shop, and a baby boutique. Finally, with the back end of the Bronco crammed to capacity, they drove to the drugstore. Buffy parked in the alley behind, and they went in through the employees' entrance. Only when Buffy was unable to hoist herself up onto a stool at the counter, did they decide to sit in a booth instead.

"You always used to order a cherry soda made with French vanilla ice cream," Buffy recalled. "Is that what you're going to get today?"

Dawn was still undecided. "Maybe, or I might get a root-beer float. That's my new favorite. What are you going to have?"

"Why don't we order one of each and share them both?"

The soda jerk, a boy of about fifteen, was new, and Buffy had to teach him how to make an ice cream soda. When the pharmacist noticed her behind the counter, he stuck his head out the dispensary window and shouted to her, "I see you're back where you belong."

"I'm not on the payroll, Doc. I'm just giving your new employ some on-the-job training."

"You know, you can come back to work here anytime you want to."

"I'll keep that in mind, but at the moment I have a job."

# XIX
# Media Attention

The Griffoun Society's Annual Black-Tie Banquet was held on the third Thursday of September in the basement conference room of Griffoun Hall, a historic building owned outright by Simon Estes. This four-story brick structure, just blocks from the University of Texas campus, was the home to Simon's used-book exchange, a coin-operated laundry, an alcohol-free pub, a members-only spa, the Griffoun Society's library and reading room, several workshops and studios associated with the club, and a dormitory for the club's co-ed volunteers, who worked in the clubhouse and posed for life classes there. The eight waitresses tonight, including Robyn and Bootsy, were all residents of that dormitory.

Simon was seated with the New Braunfels contingent at the head table. Leo had invited Buffy to attend as his guest, and she had meant to, but at the last minute, she had not felt up to the trip. Damien, a long-time member of the Griffoun Society, was seated between Mercy and Leo, the three of them having driven up together. The guests of honor, the Longs and the Flores-Hopewell clan had come in one vehicle, Abner's Suburban.

After dinner and dessert, as plates were being cleared away, Simon stepped to the lectern at the center of the head table. Whilst he spoke, welcoming guests and introducing the three young speakers, waitresses moved silently amongst the diners, placing steaming carafes on every table. Leo poured himself a cup of coffee, and sat back to listen to the program.

Simon's presentation lasted a full ten minutes. Then Jennifer walked to the lectern, and standing on a stool provided her by one of the volunteers, added a further explanation of what Dusky Nightshade's Underground Tract Society and Free Press was all about. She then yielded the floor to her step-sister, who read a yet unpublished essay. Next Verity read; then Jennifer; then Dulce again. Eventually each of the three girls read one of her own essays and at least one other by an absent member of their society. The applause was thunderous, and scores of people lined up to shake hands with the guest speakers.

After school the next day, Dawn skipped going to Leo's in favor of calling on Jennifer and Dulce. She was anxious to hear how the program had been received. Leo could have told her, but she wanted to hear it from the girls themselves.

"There must have been a million people there," Dulce hyperbolized. "I was so scared my hands were shaking."

"She did fine," Jennifer assured Dawn. "But the stool they gave us to stand on wasn't tall enough for Verity. She could barely see over the top of the lectern."

"Did everybody listen and pay attention?" Dawn wanted to know. "Did they like it?"

"They did," Jennifer said. "Lots of people were sipping coffee, but they all seemed very interested in what we had to say."

"And afterward," Verity added, "they treated us like celebrities. We autographed about a hundred copies of the magazine and shook hand till our fingers felt like they were going to fall off."

Dawn was totally amazed and said so. "I simply can't believe this. I wish I could have been there. Thanks for doing a wonderful job. You guys are the best."

A sympathetic newspaper review of the program presented by Jennifer, Dulce, and Verity attracted more attention than anyone might have imagined. Soon the names *Dusky Nightshade* and *Little Heathens* were familiar to almost everyone in Central Texas. A television station in Austin aired a brief excerpt of a cell-phone video featuring Verity addressing the multitude from behind the too-tall lectern. Then another station conducted a live in-studio interview with Jennifer and Dulce. Speculation as to the true identity of Dusky Nightshade was rife. Reverend Wainwright, in a fiery radio sermon, insisted that *Opuscule* was not the work of innocent children, but of some demonically devious adult. In early October, one of the major television networks ran a news feature on the controversy. The tone was more humorous than serious and clearly showed Darrell Wainwright for the ass he was. By the following week he had lost about thirty per cent of his congregation.

Dawn could not have been more pleased with herself.

# XX
## THE FACTS OF LIFE

Meanwhile in Houston Beryl suffered a miscarriage. No one, herself included, had even suspected that she was pregnant. Nor would she say with whom she had been sexually intimate.

"It's so silly of her to get knocked up," Mercy groused. "That school of hers has an excellent sex-education program. She should have known to take precautions."

Mercy was up in the tree house with Dawn, Starr, and Peggy. The three girls had been discussing what theme the fourth issue of their magazine should follow when Mercy had shouted for them to throw down the ladder.

"At our school," said Peggy, "they only say to wait until you're married."

"Well, abstinence is certainly the most-effective means of contraception," Mercy acknowledged. "Or at least it would be if not for the fact that so many girls absolutely determined to remain chaste until after marriage forget their good intentions in the heat of passion. Do you three know about condoms?"

Neither Starr nor Peggy had a clue what Mercy was talking about. Dawn had recently come across the word *condom* in her reading and had looked it up in the dictionary. But she still had difficulty imagining what a condom looked like and would certainly not have known how to acquire one or use it.

"I want you girls to be prepared," Mercy told them. "You may never need the protection of a condom, but not knowing about them serves no purpose consistent with your own best interest. Always remember, knowledge is power."

"We don't even have boyfriends," Starr giggled.

"That could change overnight. The time to learn how to take precautions is before you're at risk, not after."

Dawn rushed to defend her friend. "Starr didn't mean that we're not interested. We want to know everything you can tell us."

From the capacious pockets of her full skirt, Mercy produced three condoms still in their colorful wrappers. She handed them out and directed each of the girls to open one. For several minutes she allowed them to handle the condoms and get used to the look and feel of them. Then also from her pockets, she withdrew three zucchinis and instructed the girls how to unroll the condoms onto the squash. Of course, this exercise required that she explain the difference between an erect and a flaccid penis. The girls had a hundred questions, and Mercy answered them all as patiently and as honestly as she was able. It was more than an hour before she gathered up the vegetables to return them to her refrigerator.

"How old would we have to be to buy condoms?" Dawn asked.

"I really don't know," Mercy confessed. "Difficulty acquiring condoms might well be one reason Beryl engaged in unprotected sex. If only she had confided in me! Maybe she was too embarrassed or too ashamed. I just don't know. I guess I should have made a point of telling her that I buy condoms by the box and keep them in the medicine cabinet in my bathroom. She could have helped herself anytime. Do you girls understand what I'm saying?"

Dawn answered for all three. "Yes, ma'am, we do. Thank you."

That evening after supper, as Starr helped her mother do the dishes, she asked if they might have "an honest woman-to-woman talk."

"Sure, baby. What's on your mind?"

Now that Starr had the floor, she was uncertain how to proceed or even whether she should. "I know you have a boyfriend, and I was only wondering why you didn't tell me. That's all. It's not important. I'm just curious."

Suddenly Jane was terribly afraid. "How did you find out?"

Starr took a torn condom wrapper out of her pocket and tossed it on the table. "I've been seeing these in the waste basket by your bed for months. I just figured out today what they are."

"I see. Are you upset with me? Are you disappointed?"

"Of course not. I'm happy that you have a boyfriend. But why were you keeping him a secret?"

Jane bowed her head in shame. "I guess I didn't trust you. I was afraid you wouldn't approve."

"Just tell me it's not Reverend Wainwright."

Jane laughed. "Don't be ridiculous. I don't like him any more than you do."

"Who then?"

135

Jane hesitated several seconds before answering. "Damien Wynter."

Starr clapped her hands in glee. "Damien and you? I can't believe it! This is too much! Are you in love? Are you going to get married?"

Jane ignored the first question and answered only the second. "We're not going to get married. He has his life; we have ours."

Starr thought she understood. "You mean you like him for a boyfriend, but not for a husband."

"I mean that I don't think he's cut out to be a husband and a father."

"You don't think he's ready to give up his other girlfriends. Is that it?"

"You're pretty smart for an eleven-year-old."

"I'm almost twelve," Starr reminded her mother. "By the way, is it okay for me to tell Peggy and Dawn about you and Damien?"

"Let's just keep this between ourselves for now," Jane suggested.

Another important question occurred to Starr. "Do you have to buy condoms yourself? Or does Damien buy them?"

"Damien's a real gentleman. He brings his own."

"That's good, because I'll bet it would be pretty embarrassing to go into the drug store and ask for condoms Have you ever had to do that?"

"No, thank goodness, I haven't."

Later, as Starr lay abed waiting for sleep to overtake her, she began to feel guilty about all the secrets she was keeping from her mother. She was still awake when Jane looked in on her before going to bed herself.

"I have secrets too," Starr confessed. "I'd tell you if I could, but they're not my secrets alone. I've promised other people I wouldn't tell."

"Then don't. I understand completely. Good night."

# XXI
## Sin and Retribution

Everyone, of course, has secrets; most of us have at least one that cannot be shared even with those closest and dearest. Peggy, for instance, had never once confided to Dawn or to Starr that she was and had been for as long as she could remember a compulsive masturbator. Anytime she was not actively participating in some other demanding occupation, she was almost certainly engaged in auto-erotic stimulation. In church during her father's long, boring sermons she rubbed herself surreptitiously; likewise at school during long, boring lectures and alone in the back seat of the family car on long, boring trips.

For Peggy this kind of sneaky public masturbation was an act of desperation. Much more intensely satisfying was the luxurious pleasure she gave herself in private, as under the covers each night after all the lights were turned off, or better yet, in the bath, where she could be completely naked.

On a Sunday afternoon in early Autumn, Peggy, at her favorite pursuit in the upstairs bathroom of her family's home, managed to achieve a level of arousal so far beyond anything she had ever before experienced that she was not at first aware of a soft knocking at the door.

Reverend Wainwright had himself mislaid a certain reference book, but when he could not immediately put his hand on it, he naturally assumed that his irresponsible daughter had borrowed it without permission. He shouted repeatedly for her, but she did not come. Normally, on a Sunday afternoon he would have no reason whatever to venture to the upper floor, but—damn it all—he needed that book, and he needed it now. So reluctantly he climbed the stairs.

When Peggy was not to be found in her room, he tapped lightly on the bathroom door. Receiving no answer, he put his hand on the knob and was surprised to find that it would not turn. However, Peggy had failed to make certain that the door was completely shut, the bolt properly seated. Under the slight pressure of Reverend Wainwright's hand, the door swung open, revealing his only child in the lewd embrace of his archenemy Satan. It was not to be borne.

In a flash he snatched Peggy out of the tub by her upper arm. "Strumpet!" he screamed, slapping her across the face. "Harlot! Hussy! Tart! Trollop!" And with every vile epithet, he delivered another vicious blow.

Peggy was no more than a rag doll in his vise-like grip. She was helpless to defend herself, let alone escape.

Relenting at last, he flung her out the bathroom door into the hall. "Get out of my sight. Cover yourself, girl."

Peggy collided brutally with the wall opposite the bathroom and fell to the hardwood floor with a horrendous crash. Immediately she scrambled to her feet and tried to flee, but her wet feet slipped out from under her, and she fell again. In considerable pain she struggled to her hands and knees and was attempting to rise once more when her father, meaning to hurry her on her way, dealt her derriere a savage kick. The toe of his shoe connected wickedly with her perineum. Exerting herself, she managed to get to her feet, and before he could kick her again, she dashed down the hall to the relative safety of her own bedroom.

Fearing that he might decide to pursue her even here, she locked the door behind her and dressed as quickly as she was able, then raised the window and climbed out into a pear tree, which had more than once before been her escape route from the house. Upon reaching the ground, her first thought was to go to Leo. This time she would allow him to call the authorities. This time her father had gone too far. She had been terrified for her very life, and even now the throbbing between her legs made it difficult for her to walk.

In the hallway outside Peggy's room, her father was still trembling with righteous ire. He turned to go back downstairs and was felled by a massive stroke. He lay undiscovered at the top of the stairs until almost suppertime.

# XXII
## THE POLICE

**W**hen Peggy was not at school on Monday morning, Dawn and Starr assumed that she must be ill. Then when the entire student body was asked to pray for Reverend Wainwright, who was in hospital critically ill, it seemed logical to assume that Peggy was with her mother at her father's bedside. However, in the early afternoon, both Dawn and Starr were called to the principal's office, there to be interviewed by a uniformed policewoman. Were they aware that Peggy had run away? Did they have any idea where she might have gone? Had they heard from her since church yesterday morning? Had Peggy any other close friends who might know something? Neither Dawn nor Starr had anything helpful to offer.

After school Dawn rushed to Leo's apartment to tell him the news. She found him, having just returned from a weekend excursion, unpacking his suitcase.

Leo was gravely concerned. "I can understand her running away. But where would she have gone?"

"Here, I guess, to you or to Mercy."

"Mercy's in Dallas," Leo reminded her. "And I've been in Austin since Saturday."

"Maybe Buffy knows something," Dawn suggested.

"We can ask her when she comes in."

"Where is she?"

"Shopping, I suppose. The car's gone."

"May I use your phone to call Jennifer? Maybe she's heard something."

"Sure. You know where it is."

141

In less than a minute, Dawn was back at Leo's side waving a note Buffy had left by the telephone:

*Gone to hospital.*

Leo hurried to the phone and placed a call to the hospital. After his first panicky inquiries, he was connected to Buffy's room and allowed to speak to her. Buffy, he learned, had gone into labor Saturday night, called her obstetrician, then driven herself to the hospital. On Sunday morning at 5:00, she had given birth to a six-pound baby girl, whom she had named *Alba Mayfield, Mayfield* being Buffy's maiden name, which, upon leaving Bobby, she had resumed using.

Leo and Dawn, although still worried about Peggy, were so eager to see Buffy and her new daughter that they immediately set out afoot in order to get to the hospital before visiting hours ended.

"How come you don't have a car?" Dawn asked as they walked along San Antonio Street. "Don't you know how to drive?"

"I've driven most of my life, and in London I did own a car. But here I'm afraid to drive. I'm so used to driving on the left that I'd be a danger to myself and others."

"That makes sense, I suppose."

In the hospital lobby, Dawn ran into Peggy's mother and stopped to have a few words with her. Leo, pretending not to be with Dawn, walked ahead and did not look back. When Dawn got to Buffy's room, she found him there already.

"Hey, little sister," Buffy greeted her, "I'm so glad you're here. Have you seen Alba yet?"

"No, I came here first."

"Well, give me a hug; then go see her, because I want you to be her godmother."

Dawn hugged Buffy and kissed her cheek. "I didn't think I was old enough to be a godmother."

"I don't know why not. You're old enough to start your own publishing company. If anything ever happens to me, I want to know that she has somebody strong and capable to look out for her, somebody who'll love her as much I do. Leo's already agreed to be her godfather."

"I'll do it, of course, but don't you dare let anything happen to you."

Mercy's arrival from Dallas late that night solved the problem of how to get mother and baby home from hospital the next morning. Buffy could not fully appreciate the cause of everyone's concern. After all, she had driven herself to hospital; she could just as easily drive herself and her daughter home. All she would need from anyone else would be the infant carrier brought to her. Still, it was lovely to ride in the roomy back seat of Mercy's Lincoln. Risking a citation for driving without a license, Leo followed directly behind in the Bronco. Then in a queer reversal of rôles, he waited on Buffy hand and foot that afternoon, pampering her as a royal princess.

Dawn came after school and nervously held her godchild for the first time. "I can't believe how tiny she is. Did you know that the word *alba* means *dawn* in Spanish? Is that why you named her that? Or is that just a coincidence?"

Buffy smiled mysteriously. "There are no coincidences."

At feeding time, Buffy unbuttoned her blouse and nursed Alba while Dawn sat nearby watching in fascination. Leo got out his drawing pad and made sketches of the three of them. It was a happy time, but overshadowed by concern for Peggy's whereabouts and well-being.

That evening, two detectives from the Sheriff's Department (one male, the other female) called on the Ramseys at home. A search of Peggy's room earlier in the day had turned up what might well be a clue to her disappearance: a diary entry in which she mentioned the name of someone she wished she lived with instead of with her parents. Dawn knew immediately what was coming and tried to steel herself not to give anything away.

"Does the name *Leo* mean anything to you folks?" the male detective asked.

Brent and Helen both said no.

Dawn, not trusting her voice, just shook her head.

"Maybe he's someone at her school," Helen suggested.

"Or somebody in her neighborhood," Brent offered.

"Possibly," the female detective agreed, "but Ms Wainwright doesn't know him, and since Peggy spends so much time over here, we were hoping that she might have mentioned this Leo to you."

Helen could honestly say that she had never heard of anyone in New Braunfels with that name. "Maybe the Logans know him. Have you asked them?"

"We stopped by their house a minute ago," the male detective told her. "They weren't home, but we certainly intend to go back."

Dawn decided to take a chance by throwing them a red herring. "If Peggy had a boyfriend, she'd never write his real name. She'd disguise it so nobody that read it would know who she was talking about. For instance, if his name were *Billy*, she might write *Libby* instead.   Or if his initials happened to spell a name, she might just refer to him by that name."

"So this Leo might actually be *Lawrence Edward Olmstead* or something like that," the male detective speculated. "Very clever!"

"You have the makings of a great detective," the female officer told Dawn.

As soon as the two investigators were gone, Dawn called Starr to warn her not to say anything that might lead them to Leo.  Then she slipped out the back door and ran all the way to Leo's apartment.  When Leo opened the door, he was amazed to see Dawn in her nightgown and house slippers on his front porch.  She was out of breath and as pale as a sheet.

"What's happened?  Is it Peggy?"

"The cops were just at our house.  They're looking for you, but they don't know your last name yet.  Peggy wrote in her diary that she wished that she could come live with you.  They're trying to figure out who you are.  They're asking everybody if they know someone named *Leo.*"

Utterly speechless and totally deflated, Leo sat down on the ottoman.  His hands were trembling at the prospect of falling into the clutches of a constabulary already half convinced that he had abducted or harmed a child.

"I have to go now," Dawn said.  "My parents don't know I'm gone."

"Yes, of course, go," Leo urged.  "And thank you for coming.  You may have saved my life."

Leo tapped softly on Buffy's bedroom door, and when she opened it to him, he related to her this latest development.

"Oh, God!" she exclaimed. "This is a fucking nightmare. What are we going to do?"

"I don't know, but I don't intend to be here when the police arrive. Do me a favor. Call Mercy. Ask her to come down. I'm going to need her to drive me to San Antonio."

Mercy was dressed and downstairs in less than five minutes, by which time Leo was packed and ready to go. He signed a few blank checks on an account that had several thousand dollars in it and handed the checkbook to Buffy along with special instructions in the event he was never able to return. Then he kissed her good-bye and was gone.

On Wednesday afternoon, when Dawn called, she found Mercy loading all of Leo's paintings into a rental van.

"What's going on? Where's Leo?" she demanded.

"Leo's out of town for a while. When this trouble blows over, he'll come home to us. By the way, he wanted you to have a painting. He said that by modeling for him you'd earned it many times over."

"Which painting?"

"Whichever one you want."

"Even a big one?"

"He didn't mention any restrictions. Let Buffy or me know which one you want, and we'll hang onto it for you until you're able to take possession of it."

"That might not be till I'm grown."

"I know. In the meantime, why don't you pitch in and give me a hand putting these in the truck?"

"Oh, sure. Where are you taking them?"

In fact, Mercy had rented a warehouse unit. She knew that it was just a matter of days at most before investigators would locate Leo's apartment, and she did not wish the pictures to fall into their hands. For one thing, it might be difficult to get them back. And for another, she could just imagine mean-spirited policemen trying to identify all Leo's models, calling on them at home, asking pointless but embarrassing questions in front of their families.

With two people working, the paintings were quickly loaded. Before leaving for the warehouse, however, Mercy suggested that they walk through the apartment one last time to make certain they were not leaving behind anything they would not care to have found. Dawn immediately thought of Leo's typed homilies and his private journal.

"Leo mentioned those specifically," Buffy told her. "He wanted me to turn them over to his publisher."

"His publisher?"

"Dusky Nightshade, of course."

Dawn turned to Mercy. "May I keep them in the warehouse for the time being?"

"No problem. Now let's get out of here."

On the way to the warehouse, Dawn asked Mercy to advise her on a personal matter. "I mean, you know a lot about men, right? You've probably had dozens of boyfriends in your life."

Mercy was already more than a little amused. "A few."

"How do you get somebody to like you?"

"You don't, Dawn. Either he likes you or he doesn't. You just have to be yourself and let nature take its own course."

"But I can't quit thinking about him. And he doesn't even notice me. It's driving me crazy."

"Dawn, are you still panting after Duane?"

Dawn blushed down to the tips of her toes. Had she been so obvious? "I thought I was over him

147

last summer, but I keep running into him at the grocery store and other places. It just feels like I'm going to die if he doesn't kiss me."

"Do you have any idea how much trouble a grown man can get into by allowing himself to become romantically involved with a girl your age? He could go to prison for the rest of his life. Would you really want to subject Duane to that kind of risk?"

"Of course not. I guess I just didn't think it through very well."

"Stick to boys your own age, at least till you're eighteen. After that, it doesn't matter so much."

Thank goodness, Mercy thought to herself, that Dawn had not developed just such a crush on Damien or Leo. The two of them were so bewitched by her that had she thrown herself at either of them, he might not have had the will power to resist her advances.

"Mercy," Dawn asked, "do you think Leo will ever come back?"

"He will if he can, I'm sure. I just hope he can."

Tears came immediately to Dawn's eyes. "You think something really bad has happened to Peggy, don't you?"

"No, I don't think anything yet, but it is a possibility."

At school on Thursday, Starr confided to Dawn that her mother was thinking about enrolling her in public school next semester. "She's totally fed up with Reverend Wainwright and all his screwy notions."

"Maybe my parents will finally see the light too. At least, I hope so."

"I suppose you noticed, we already quit going to church."

"I figured your mom was sick or something."

"Sick of religion, that's all. She calls it the 'crock of ages.'"

"Are you going to start going to some other church?"

"Could be. I don't know."

"You could tell your mom about that freethinkers' fellowship that Brenda's parents belong to. Cibolo wouldn't be too far to drive."

Starr shrugged indifferently. "We'll see. For now I like sleeping in on Sunday."

When Dawn got home that afternoon, she changed into play clothes, made herself a snack, then set out to call on Buffy. From a block away, however, she could see police cars in the driveway. She made an abrupt about-face, returned home, and called Starr to let her know that Leo's full identity had been uncovered. Almost as an afterthought, she called Jennifer. The police might now be able to start making all kinds of connections. It was not unlikely that members of the Flores-Hopewell and the Long households would soon be interviewed by detectives.

For the next hour or so, Dawn remained on pins and needles. Finally she could bear it no longer and dialed Mercy's number.

"Hello."

"This is Dawn. Are you alone?"

"Yes, the police were here, but they've left. I imagine you'll be seeing them tonight. They know now that you lied to them about not knowing Leo."

Dawn felt blindsided. "You told them?"

149

"In the studio they found photographs taken at the party of you and him and the other girls in a group. I tried to tell them that you had probably never heard Leo's first name, that to you he was simply *Mr Madrigal, Brenda's grandfather*, but I don't think they believed me."

"Well, I guess it could be worse."

"I'm afraid it is worse. In the tree house, they found hand-written documents related to your publishing enterprise. Unless they are more inept than we dare hope, they will soon have everyone's alias matched to her true identity. One way or another, your parents are soon going to find out everything."

"So the secret's out. In a way, I'm glad. When Mom started repeating what Reverend Wainwright was saying, that Dusky Nightshade is really an adult pretending to be an eleven-year-old, I was right on the verge of telling her the truth. Now I can."

Mercy took a deep breath and let it out slowly. "There's one more thing I have to tell you. It's pretty bad."

"How bad?"

"They found a pair of Peggy's undies in the trash can behind the garage. They had blood on them, lots of blood."

A wave of dizziness swept over Dawn. The receiver slipped from her hand as darkness clouded her vision. For a second or two, she remained standing, even though she was completely unconscious. Then she poled over, striking her head on a cast-iron umbrella stand.

"Dawn! Are you there? Talk to me." Mercy suspected what had happened and cursed herself for having delivered such dire news over the telephone. Unable to get a dial tone, she dashed down the hall

150

to her bedroom, where her cell phone was charging. Without bothering to unplug it, she dialed Helen at the bookstore and urged her to hurry home to see about Dawn. Then she ran out to her car and drove to the Ramsey house, where she found both front and back doors locked. It seemed an eternity before Helen arrived.

Inside they found Dawn on the hall floor no longer unconscious, but in a confused stupor. Helen knelt and wept and held her daughter to her. Mercy stepped into the bathroom and wet a washcloth to put on Dawn's forehead.

"Somebody bonked me on the head," Dawn asserted. "I was talking to Mercy on the phone, and a burglar must have come up behind me."

"No, no," Mercy laughed. "You just fainted. You must have smacked your head when you fell."

Helen began examining the bump on Dawn's head. "I think we should have you checked out by a doctor."

"Oh, no!" Dawn said, covering her face with both hands.

Helen was baffled. "Don't be so silly. You've never been afraid of going to the doctor."

"It's not that. I just remembered what Mercy told me about Peggy."

Helen turned to Mercy. "What about Peggy?"

Mercy sighed heavily. "The police found a pair of underpants belonging to her, underpants with extensive blood stains on them."

"Oh, no!" Helen gasped. "Oh, no!"

"But they can't be sure they belong to Peggy," Dawn argued. "Can they?"

"They're pretty sure. It seems that when Peggy went to camp last year, her mother put her name in the waistbands of all her undies, and those they found match. A laboratory will have to determine whether it's Peggy's blood or not. But even if it is, that doesn't necessarily mean—you know. There could be some simple explanation. Let's not give up hope yet."

Dawn was still shaky, and her knees were weak as Helen and Mercy helped her to the car. When it began to look as though Mercy meant to accompany them to the emergency room, Dawn firmly stated that she needed to be alone with her mother. "There's something I have to talk to her about, and it's very urgent."

Dawn's disclosure and the grilling that followed lasted throughout the drive to the hospital. Helen was at first incredulous, then hurt and angry. Dawn was unrepentant. The grilling resumed three hours later on the way home. Helen accused Dawn of betraying her family by attacking everything most dear to them and utilizing their own resources to do it.

"That's not how I see it," Dawn countered. "I only did what I thought was right. I used my birthday money, which was mine alone. And I used my allowance, which you give me, true enough, but as soon as you do, it becomes mine to do with as I see fit."

"Not any longer. As of today, your allowance is canceled, and your computer is going into the kitchen, where I can keep an eye on what you're up to. You're not to touch it unless I am in the room. Is that clear?"

"Oh, it's clear alright. It's just not fair."

"When you're grown up and have a family of your own, you can decide what's fair. Until then, it's my responsibility, and I take my responsibilities seriously."

152

Helen immediately resigned her job at the bookstore, offering only an abject apology in lieu of two weeks' notice, and withdrew Meghan from afternoon day care. Henceforth, she would spend more time with both her daughters, instilling character, imparting Christian values, and overseeing their daily activities.

Mercy, meanwhile, had hatched a theory that Reverend Wainwright might accidentally have slain Peggy, then tried to frame Leo by planting her bloody underwear in that garbage can. "He's a violent man," she told Buffy, "but he would never deliberately kill anyone, let alone his own child. And yet, in one of his rages, he might have struck her too hard. Then for him to attempt to put the blame elsewhere seems not at all unlikely."

"You should go to the police with this," Buffy advised. "I'll bet they don't know what kind of man he really is."

"Cops don't like help from amateur sleuths, I should imagine. But they can't ignore the photographs I have. They'll have to brace Wainwright about his habitual mistreatment of Peggy. We'll see where that leads."

The detective in charge of the case was named *Branson*. Mercy made an appointment to see him in person in his office.

After examining the photographs of Peggy's welts and bruises, he demanded to know, "Why didn't you bring these to someone's attention months ago?"

"I did what I believed to be in Peggy's best interest. If that's a crime, arrest me. I assure you, I can afford the best lawyers money can buy."

Branson waved his hand dismissively. "Oh, hell! I ain't fixing to arrest you. I'll keep these photos, if you don't mind, not that they're likely to do me much good.  Preacher Wainwright's been in the hospital since the day Peggy went missing.  He's no more than a vegetable, and the doctors don't give him much chance of getting any better.  If we're ever going to know what happened, we're going to have to find Peggy.  And we surely would like to have a word with your downstairs neighbor."

Dawn found herself overwhelmed these days by negative emotions.  When she was not worrying about Peggy, she was worrying about Leo.  She was in no mood to write or publish anything, but she bridled at being denied to right to do so.  She chaffed at the loss of her allowance and resented the "unjust" restrictions imposed upon her personal liberty. While she did her chores without complaint, even doing more than was required of her, she went about with a perpetual scowl on her face.  She always made it a point to be polite, but just barely.  Friendliness was out of the question.  If called to task for glowering at her mother, she apologized frostily and promised to try not to let her true feelings show through again.

Her dour mood seemed to infect the very atmosphere of the Ramsey home.  As the weeks passed, this household, once happy and nurturing, grew gloomier and gloomier.  Soon Helen and Brent were both as deeply mired in depression as was Dawn.  Only Meghan seemed unchanged.  And how long could that remain so?

The first stage of the siege endured until the day before Halloween, when Helen made the first tentative offer of a negotiated peace.  "What would it take to put an honest smile on your face again, Dawn?"

"I'll smile when I'm grown up and I can have a life of my own."

"Your father and I have been talking. Maybe we could reinstate your allowance. Would that help?"

"Do whatever you think is right. I'm sure you will anyway."

Helen threw up her hands and stormed out of the room. "It's so exasperating trying to talk to you!"

Dawn leapt up from the sofa and followed her mother into the kitchen. "Yeah? Well, what's the point of talking when nobody's listening?"

Helen whirled about to face Dawn. "I'm listening now. What do you want?"

"I want to be out of here. Out of this house; it's a prison. And out of this family. I hate my life!"

Helen burst into tears, and it was all that Dawn could do to resist the instinct to put her arms around her and try to comfort her. Instead, she turned and stalked away to shut herself in her room.

Fifteen minutes later Helen rapped on Dawn's bedroom door, then stepped inside without waiting for an invitation. "Will you answer me one question?"

Dawn was lying on her bed. She sat up and put her feet on the floor. "What do you want to know? I've already confessed to everything I've ever done."

"Do you love us?"

Dawn chewed her lower lip. "Maybe. I don't know. I love Meghan."

"Do you know that we love you?"

"That's two questions."

"Give me a break, Dawn. Just answer. Do you believe me when I tell you that your father and I love you?"

"Yeah, I suppose so, in your own little way."

"You think we should love you more? Is that it? If only we loved you enough, we wouldn't set limits or make rules?"

"Rules are for robots. I'm a person, and I can set my own limits. I should think a good parent would understand that."

"You don't think I'm a good parent?"

Dawn could see that her mother was terribly hurt, but this was not the time for ruth. "Not very."

"Then whom should I emulate? Can you name someone you think is a good parent?"

"Sure. Lots of people. But you don't know most of them."

"Well, let's just talk about the ones I do know."

"Okay then, Brenda's mother, Carmen, but I guess you don't know her very well. Also Mercy. She's not actually a parent, but if she were, she'd be a really good example. And Ms Logan; she may not be perfect, but she's a lot better mother than you are."

Helen was steamed. "Sometimes, Dawn, I'd just like to slap you silly."

"Go ahead if it'll make you feel better. But honestly, Mom, why ask the question if you don't want to hear the answer?"

Helen turned and left the room, slamming the door behind her.

The next day, Helen bought Dawn a Halloween mask in hopes that she could talk her into trick-or-treating with Meghan. Meghan had picked out her own mask and costume a week ago and was eagerly looking forward to tonight.

"I'll take Meghan if you want to stay home," Dawn offered, "but I'm not interested for myself, and I won't wear a mask."

"I'm taking Meghan," Helen said firmly. "You're welcome to come along with or without a mask. Or you can stay home and pass out candy at the door. It's up to you."

"That's Dad's job. He likes seeing all the little kids in their costumes. I think I'll just take a shower and go to bed early."

The next morning at breakfast, Meghan was still talking about the night before. "But why wouldn't Peggy say hi to me?"

"I told you last night, sugarplum, it wasn't Peggy."

"Yes, it was. I said, 'Hi, Peggy,' and she just walked away. Why's she mad at me? I didn't do anything to her."

Dawn's curiosity was aroused. "What's she talking about, Mom?"

"We passed a girl in a gorilla mask, and your sister thought it was Peggy."

"It was Peggy," Meghan insisted. "And she wasn't wearing a gorilla mask; she was wearing a werewolf mask."

To Meghan, Dawn asked, "If she had on a mask, how did you know who she was?"

"I could just tell. That's all."

Dawn wanted to believe, and part of her mind was almost persuaded by Meghan's certainty. But why would Peggy be playing at such a game? It made no sense at all.

# XXIII
## LIFE AS A FUGITIVE

B eyond the Rio Grande, Leo was becoming more anxious by the week. He had hoped by now to have received the all-clear signal from Carmen. It was maddening not to know what was going on back home. And yet there was no one he dared to contact. If he stayed away much longer, he would have to devise some means of earning a living. His savings had been considerable, but they were dwindling away fast.

Leo had now so drastically altered his appearance that not even his own mother would have recognized him, or so he told himself. He had crossed into Mexico looking very much the wealthy American tourist. Today his appearance was that of a native peon. He was scruffy, unshaven, and dirty. His clothes—not the ones he had left New Braunfels wearing—were in tatters. He carried his belongings in a filthy burlap bag. He kept no identity papers on his person, and he made a point never to speak English or let it be guessed that he understood English. He was as nearly invisible as it is possible for a person to be.

As a further precaution, he stayed on the move, crisscrossing the country by bus and by train. Once a week he tried to pass through some major city, where he could buy the Sunday *Times*. There was a certain risk involved in doing so, but he felt he had to take that risk, for it was through an ad in the *Times* that Carmen might someday summon him home.

Buffy, in Leo's absence, grew closer and closer to Mercy, who called on her at least once a day. In Buffy's room—the room she shared with Alba—she had a tiny portable television with rabbit ears. It was the only television in the apartment, and for the longest time, it was her only entertainment. Then somehow she became interested in Leo's books, and almost overnight reading replaced television as her primary pastime. Determined to get back into shape as quickly as possible, she pursued a vigorous exercise regimen. She missed Dawn frightfully, but having been informed by Mercy of what Dawn was going through, she could only hope that the situation might someday improve.

Grounded indefinitely, Dawn felt cut off from everything she cared about and from everyone she liked the most. She was not even allowed to associate with Starr, save at school. She saw Mercy occasionally, but only in her mother's presence. In deep frustration, she managed to secretly post a letter conferring management responsibility of her entire publishing operation to Jennifer. At school she urged Starr to contact Jennifer and Dulce and to be as helpful as she could. But Starr had lost interest in writing and publishing. It seemed that *Opuscule* was finished after only three issues.

That was not, in fact, the case. Jennifer was bubbling over with new ideas and eager to implement them. She had never really stopped working on Issue Number Four. Nor had she given Dulce and Verity time to lose interest, as Starr had done. Jennifer had even been in touch with Beryl and Brenda, both of whom were now working on new assignments. Dawn's letter only formalized the transfer of power that had already taken place.

In the Ramsey home, the stand-off continued. Helen was so discouraged by the response to her first peace offering that she was reluctant to try again. And yet things simply must not remain as they were. There were signs now that even Meghan was beginning to be affected. Brent wanted to send Dawn to a child psychologist, but Helen was distrustful of the mental-health profession, which she perceived as hostile to religion. The breaking point came when Meghan, her little face grimly serious, asked Helen why she and Dawn had quit liking each other. "Are you going to quit liking me someday too?"

Helen, of course, broke down in tears and hugged Meghan to her, protesting vehemently that she would never stop loving either of her daughters. "Dawn and I just aren't getting along right now. We'll work out our differences soon, and things will be like they used to be."

Meghan shook her head sadly. "I don't think so,"

At this point Helen was prepared to surrender unconditionally. She approached Dawn one last time. Tapping on the bedroom door, she asked, "Can we talk?"

"Okay," said Dawn, "but this time I get to ask the questions."

"That seems fair. What do you want to know?"

"Whom do you love more, me or—"

"Don't even say it, Dawn," Helen interrupted. "You can't possibly be jealous of Meghan. We love both our daughters equally. Surely you know that."

"That's not what I was going to ask. I wouldn't even blame you if you did love her more. I don't care about that."

"Well, we don't love her more, not one bit more, and not one bit less either."

"Alright, alright, I believe you. Just let me finish? Whom do you love more, me or God?"

Helen looked as though she had been struck. "It's not the same, Dawn. You can't compare parental devotion to worshipful adoration."

"I'll bet Reverend Wainwright can. Maybe you should call him up and ask his opinion."

"Let's keep this strictly between us. Okay?"

"I wish. You're the one who's always dragging us to his stupid church, listening to his stupid advice, making me go to his stupid school. What do you think when he preaches about Abraham and his son, which he does about once a month, or Jeptha and his daughter. Do you ever ask yourself whether you love God as much as they did?"

Helen shook her head in denial, but could not immediately find her voice to answer.

Dawn clearly had the upper hand, but relented. "Look, don't worry about it. I figured out years ago that God meant more to you that I did. I don't think it's right, but it's no big deal."

"Oh, Dawn, I had no idea. Listen to me. Maybe we are supposed to love our Creator more than we love our children. If that's the case, then I'm afraid I fail pretty badly as a servant of God. I could never do what Jeptha did. So I guess that means I love you more."

Dawn had been rehearsing this conversation for days; she knew exactly how to respond. "You love me more than you love God, but still not enough to respect me for who I am. You think you can make me into the person you want me to be."

"That's not true at all. I only want you to be the best you that you can be. When you were only a week old, your father and I stood at the altar with you

161

and swore a sacred oath 'to teach you by precept and example.' Would you have us break that oath?"

"I belong to me, not to you."

"Okay, okay, this is getting us nowhere. But at least we're talking. Right? So what would it take to make you happy?"

"You really want to know?"

"Yes, really."

"Alright, I'll tell you. I want my allowance back, and I want my computer. I want to go to public school, and I want to be able to choose my own friends. I want to be free to go to whatever church I like or not go to any church at all if I don't feel like it. I want to be able to read any book that interests me and go to any movie they'll sell me a ticket to. And I want to start publishing again. I have lots to say that needs to be said."

"That's quite a list,"

"One more thing, I want Internet too, but only if we can afford it. Or maybe I can pay for it out of my allowance. I don't know how much it costs."

Helen laughed. "I appreciate your being so considerate of our tight budget."

"You could go back to work, you know. It was silly to quit over nothing."

"Is that another demand—that I go back to work—or just a helpful suggestion?"

"It's only a suggestion. I like being on my own in the afternoon. It's peaceful around here with nobody else at home. But it's not enough to make me happy or unhappy."

"Let me see if I have this straight. You want your allowance, your computer with Internet, your own friends, your own church, public school. What else?"

"No censorship and the right to publish again."

"And if we agree to all these demands, you'll be gloriously happy."

"Yes."

"And what if we feel we simply can't do everything you ask? Are some items on your list more important than others? If we can't make you gloriously happy, what would it take to make you not quite so unhappy?"

"See? I knew you'd pull something like this. Just do whatever you're going to do, and leave me out of it."

"We're negotiating, Dawn."

"How can I negotiate? You have all the power."

"How about if we put this to a neutral third party? I don't want to be unreasonable, and I'm sure you don't either."

"This doesn't have anything to do with reasonable and unreasonable. You asked what would make me happy. That's not negotiable. How could it be?"

"You don't have to be happy to act happy. I'd settle for your sincere promise to be outwardly cheerful again."

"Forget it. I'm not that good an actress. Now, if you don't mind, I'd like to be alone."

"Alright, I'll go, but I want you to do one thing for me. Write out your list of demands on a piece of paper. I'll discuss them with your father tonight, and I don't want to leave anything out."

Helen, of course, had no intention of bringing Dawn's demands to her husband's attention. He trusted her to make all decisions related to the home. Her ruling in this matter would be final, and her inclination was simply to acquiesce to the entire list. That would certainly be the easiest course of action and probably the only one sure to return peace and

163

harmony to the household. But Helen needed to believe that by doing so, she would not necessarily become a bad parent. And so she sought advice from Mercy.

"This is so surprising," Mercy said. "Sulking and pouting are not behaviors I would have expected from Dawn."

"It's much more than sulking and pouting. She's utterly and hopelessly miserable, and she blames me for all her unhappiness. She's working herself up to hate me. And it's destroying our family."

"I can't tell you what to do, Helen, but I do have a few thoughts I can share with you. First, as regards her allowance, she is a member of your family and will be until she's grown. As such, she is entitled to a share of the family's income. Whether or not you have a responsibility to place restrictions on the way she spends her allowance is another matter. My feeling is that it isn't really hers unless she has the right to spend it however she chooses."

"I guess I can go along with that."

"Now, let's consider censorship. Dealing with the Internet will be relatively easy. Just set her browser for safe search and then lock that setting with a password. I seriously doubt that she will even notice. If she does and objects, send her to me. I'll quickly set her straight."

Helen laughed. "Now, that I'd like to see."

"When it comes to books, however, there is absolutely no way you can impose any censorship whatever without incurring her resentment. And if she has any freedom of movement, she'll simply find a way around whatever restrictions you place on her reading. On the other hand, if you grant her the right to read anything that appeals to her and she knows that you are not going to renege on the agreement, then you can ask her to keep you informed about what she's reading, and you can have frank discussions about it."

"And what if it's pornographic? Am I seriously supposed to sit down with her and have a conversation about *Candy* or *Fanny Hill?*"

"Without actually forbidding her to read books like that, you could explain to her your objections to that type of literature. I believe that that is the only way you can hope to have any influence on her reading. The same goes for movies. Likewise for the friends she chooses."

"I don't know if I can do this."

"It requires no great courage or wisdom to do what's easy. But when you do something difficult, you become a better person yourself."

"And the vow I made at Dawn's baptism, how can I forget that?"

"That vow contained the phrase *until she reaches years of discretion*. Is that not so?"

Helen nodded. "I think so. Yes."

"And has she not reached years of discretion? Unless I am mistaken, she's now old enough to choose to become a member of your church."

"She refuses to even consider doing so."

"Helen, you're missing the point. If the church would allow her to join, it is because she is deemed to have reached years of discretion. You have fulfilled your vow. You are no longer under that particular obligation. The greatest service you can do her now is to trust her to make her own decisions."

Helen was dubious. "She's still a child, Mercy."

"And she'll continue to need your support and protection for a few more years, but you no longer have to think for her. She's quite capable of thinking for herself.  Allow her to be obedient to her own conscience."

Helen sighed deeply.  "I guess I know what I have to do, but it feels like I'm giving up on everything I believe in."

"Have you ever read any of the literature Dawn published?"

"No, I heard about it.  That's all."

"You should read it.  And even if you don't agree with all of it, I don't see how you could fail to be proud of her."

"It seems to me that Brenda's grandfather must have put her up to writing those articles and told her what to say?"

Mercy shook her head adamantly.  "Dawn's opinions are her own.  No one can tell her what to think, and no one can put words in her mouth. What's more, the idea to publish was her own.  Of that I am certain."

Although taken completely by surprise, Dawn accepted her mother's capitulation with the same graciousness shown Lee by Grant at Appomattox.  Indeed, Helen would afterward congratulate herself on having achieved a diplomatic solution, conveniently forgetting that she had, in a contest of wills, been bested by a not-quite-twelve-year-old.

Dawn was eager to go see Buffy and Alba, but she was scrupulous to extend her mother the courtesy of asking permission first.

"Remind me who these people are," Helen said.

"Buffy is a girl who used to work at the drugstore downtown. Last year she got married, but now she's divorced. Alba is her baby, and I'm the godmother, which is because Buffy thinks of me as her little sister."

"You're the baby's godmother? How remarkable! Would it be possible, do you think, for me to meet Buffy and Alba?"

"Oh, sure. Buffy's really nice, and Alba's the sweetest baby you ever saw." Suddenly Dawn was struck with a terrific idea. "Hey! I know. Let's ask them over for Thanksgiving dinner next week. We could invite Mercy too."

"Would you really like that?" Helen asked.

"More than anything."

"Then be sure to tell them that the invitation comes from me too."

That evening after supper, Dawn called Jennifer and Dulce and then Verity to invite them to her house on Saturday. She was anxious for her mother to meet her new friends and be reassured that they were all nice girls. She was ready to get back to work and eager to hear what Jennifer had been doing with the publishing operation whilst she herself had been on restriction. Almost as an afterthought, she called Starr and asked her to come too. Starr had once been editress-in-chief. Just possibly she could be enticed back to her old job. In any case, Dawn meant to try.

Dawn had originally conceived *Dusky Nightshade's Opuscule* as a quarterly periodical. Jennifer, feeling that the Little Heathens would soon run out of suitable fresh material, proposed redefining it as a finite series of fascicles, all of which could be kept in a single loose-leaf binder. The exact number of fascicles that would constitute the complete work might be in the range of ten to thirteen. Jennifer had even drawn up a list of possible themes. Dawn liked the idea and approved it out of hand. Jennifer would now become project directress for *Opuscule*, freeing Dawn to concentrate on book publishing. Dulce was given the responsibility of organizing a new division devoted to multimedia production.

For the Thanksgiving feast at the Ramsey home, Buffy contributed four homemade pies: one mince, one pecan, and two of pumpkin. Mercy brought a large spiral-cut honey-cured ham and two bottles of a sparkling non-alcoholic wine. The unchallenged belle of the occasion was Alba, who

was on her best behavior and charmed everyone. She made a particular conquest of Brent by seeming to prefer his lap to all others. Then she obligingly fell asleep just as dinner was served.

Later, whilst Mercy and Dawn helped with the clean-up, Buffy took Alba to Dawn's bedroom to change her diaper and then to nurse her. Meghan, the only witness, would thereafter, to the mild embarrassment of some in that household, incorporate into her games of make-believe the very realistic pretense of breast-feeding her baby dolls.

Only when the kitchen was sparkling clean again and all the leftovers had been put away, did Helen serve coffee and pie in the living room. Dawn's job was to take pie orders and to dollop out whipped cream for those who wanted it. In the midst of these festivities, the telephone rang, and Helen asked Dawn to go answer it. Mercy had just told a funny story; so Dawn had to choke back her laughter in order to say hello.

"Who is this? Is Mercy there?"

Dawn recognized the voice immediately. "Peggy, is that you?"

"Dawn? What are you doing at Mercy's house on Thanksgiving Day? I thought you'd be at home with your family."

"I am. Mercy's here too. She must have put her phone on call-forwarding. Where are you? Everybody's been worried to death."

"I'm okay. I'll see you soon. But right now, I need to talk to Mercy."

"I'll get her, but you have to tell the police that Leo didn't kidnap you or anything."

"I know. I know. I just found out that they think he did. That's why I'm calling. I need Mercy to pick me up and take me there, so I don't have to talk to them alone."

Mercy spoke briefly on the telephone with Peggy, then left to go meet her. Dawn wanted to ride along, but Mercy said no. Less than an hour later, Mercy was back alone.

"What happened?" Dawn demanded. "Wasn't she there?"

"Oh, yes. I picked her up and took her home to her mother. She can talk to the police tomorrow or later tonight if they can't wait. I should call them now and let them know what's going on."

Mercy telephoned the number on Detective Branson's card and got an answering service. She left him a message that could not be ignored. Branson returned her call within five minutes. Mercy brought him up to date, and he agreed that tomorrow would be soon enough for Peggy to be interviewed. He was enjoying a football game at the moment and did not care to work on a holiday unless absolutely required to. He did, however, feel duty bound to call Ms Wainwright for confirmation that Peggy was indeed safe at home.

# XXIV
## Peggy's Story

After escaping her father's wrath by climbing out her bedroom window, Peggy had gone straightaway to Leo's apartment, but no one had been home there. So she had rung Mercy's doorbell, again with no response. Intending to wait for either Leo or Mercy to return home, she had climbed up into the tree house and promptly fallen asleep in the window seat. She had awakened after dark and found Leo's and Mercy's apartments still deserted. She might have waited there all night had she not been so cold and so hungry. Behind the garage, after removing her jeans and underwear, she had squatted to urinate on the ground. Only then had she noticed all the blood on her panties, blood that had resulted, no doubt, from her father's having kicked her from behind. She had tossed the ruined garment into the nearby garbage can and put her jeans back on. At this point Peggy had formulated a new plan of action. She had walked to a public telephone and called Toby, who had been only too happy to hear from her.

"Meet me at the railroad trestle over the Comal River," he had instructed her. "I think I know where I can hide you."

Toby's family owned a dozen tourist cabins in a dense wood near Landa Park. It was Toby's responsibility to maintain these cabins. Throughout the summer months, all the units stayed occupied, but for the remainder of the year, most stood vacant. True, a few might be rented during Wurstfest, but never more than half of them.

171

So it was here that Toby had taken Peggy, to the cabin farthest from the riverfront, the cabin least likely to be rented. He had visited her every day, brought her food, magazines, books, sheets and blankets, a radio, a portable television, and several changes of clothes. For about a week, their relationship had remained chaste, but as they had become more comfortable with each other, well, you know how one thing leads to another. Eventually they had fallen deeply in love. A tentative first kiss had led to more kisses, and kisses had quickly escalated to petting, at which point Peggy had suggested that before Toby's next visit, he should make an effort to acquire some condoms. And that, dear Reader, is all that I intend to say about the intimacy between those two.

Toby had faithfully delivered the news of Reverend Wainwright's stroke and had even suggested that Peggy might wish to return home for her mother's sake.

"I'd rather stay here with you," she had told him.

Soon, however, boredom had set in, and Peggy had started missing her friends. At Halloween, in a mask provided by Toby, she had ventured into public, hoping to find some opportunity to communicate privately with Starr or with Dawn. She had seen neither of them, but had herself been seen and somehow recognized by Meghan. Peggy had promptly fled back to the safety of her cabin, and there she might have remained until summer had not Toby brought her the disturbing news that the police and FBI were searching for one Leo Madrigal in connection with her disappearance. That very day she had quitted the cabin forever. From a public phone at Warneke's she had called Mercy to collect her and take her to the police station.

As much as Peggy dreaded talking to the detectives, she dreaded returning home. She felt no affection whatever for her father, and very little for her mother, who had never lifted a finger to protect her from her father's harsh discipline. She was in no way prepared for the tearful hugs and kisses her mother showered on her. From her badly crippled father, she received neither welcome nor acknowledgment. But she no longer feared him. In any kind of physical confrontation, she felt confident that she could get the better of him.

Peggy's debriefing by Detective Branson the following morning was less grueling than she had feared it might be. The story she told was as close to the absolute truth as possible without revealing Toby's involvement with her. She had to repeat it twice.

Branson scratched his head. "There's just one little detail I don't quite understand, Peggy. What did you eat all this time?"

"Just regular food."

Branson laughed. "But where did you get it? I mean, somebody must have been bringing you groceries. Who was it?"

"Nobody helped me," Peggy insisted. "I found a few cans in the pantry. Somebody must have left them there last summer."

"That's easy to believe, and it probably lasted you two or three days. What did you do after that? Did you buy food? And if so, where? And how did you get money? Or did you trade for it?"

"I didn't buy, because I didn't have any money, and I didn't trade, because I didn't have anything to trade with."

"And yet you didn't starve, did you?"

"There were a few days I didn't eat." This was an outright lie. Thanks to Toby, she had never missed a meal.

"What are you trying to hide?" Branson pressed her. "Why won't you tell me what I want to know?"

Peggy crossed her arms stubbornly. "I have the right to remain silent."

"No, you don't," Branson contradicted her. "You're not under arrest. You're not even under suspicion for any crime."

"But I still don't have to incriminate myself. It's in the Constitution."

Branson threw up his hands in frustration. "Hell's bells, girl! Nobody's asking you to incriminate yourself. Just tell me who gave you food."

Mercy felt the need to intervene. "Detective, what if nobody gave her food? She said that she did what she had to do. Don't you think it's likely that she was forced to resort to stealing?"

Peggy opened her mouth to protest, but Mercy's stern look shut her up.

Branson was beginning to regret having allowed Mercy to be in the room. "Peggy, is that what happened? I can guarantee you immunity from prosecution if that's what you're worried about."

Peggy took a deep breath, stalling for time, trying to decide whether to stand pat or complicate her story with another lie. She glanced at Mercy, then at the female detective, who had so far stood quietly against the far wall. Finally she told Branson, "I have nothing more to say."

Mercy stood and took Peggy's hand. "I guess we're through then. If Detective Branson has any further questions, he can put them to your lawyer."

"But I don't have a lawyer."

"You will in less than an hour. Let's go talk to one."

Branson heaved himself to his feet. "Never mind that. I withdraw the question. But I am going to insist that Peggy be checked out by a doctor."

Mercy started to object, but Branson cut her off. "I've already settled this with Ms Wainwright. You're only here in her place because she felt she had to stay with her sick husband."

That very afternoon Peggy was subjected to a thorough physical examination, including blood work and her first-ever pelvic exam. The doctor confirmed the existence of a fresh scar on Peggy's perineum consistent with her claim to have been kicked by her father. No semen was found in her vagina. Nor had she any STD. The absence of a hymen was suggestive of a sexual assault, but hardly conclusive. And so the matter was closed.

Peggy was overjoyed to be reunited with her girlfriends, and they were relieved beyond words to have her back amongst them. During her absence, she had written no less than twelve essays, which she now turned over to Dawn. Those that seemed apropos to themes scheduled to be covered in *Opuscule* Dawn passed on to Starr. The rest she filed for possible use in the future.

Peggy and Toby, although as deeply in love as ever, had agreed that it would be prudent for them not to have any contact with each other for some little while. It simply would not do to draw attention to their forbidden relationship. And of this relationship Peggy breathed not a word to anyone.

From Mercy, Carmen received news of Peggy's miraculous reappearance and immediately started running in the Sunday *Times* an ad containing a password known only to her and to Leo. This was the signal that it was safe for him to call her. On the telephone, she could then relate to him in detail the situation he would be facing upon his return. Three weeks later she would still not have heard from him.

Ms Wainwright, who had never in her adult life made any decision more important than what to prepare for supper, now deferred to Peggy's judgment as she had once deferred to her husband's. For about two weeks after her homecoming, Peggy watched her mother struggle to care for the now-invalid Reverend Wainwright at home. Finally Peggy put her foot down and demanded that her father be placed in the care of a nursing facility.

Ms Wainwright merely asked, "Do you really think that's necessary, Peggy?"

"Yes, Mother, I do," Peggy answered firmly.

Ms Wainwright made no further argument, but simply called a social worker, who had long been urging the same course of action.

Encouraged by how easily she had prevailed, Peggy announced to her mother that after the Christmas holidays, in order to save money, she would be attending public school.

"I suppose that's best," Ms Wainwright conceded. "But your father certainly would be disappointed."

As Christmas approached, Dawn asked Buffy for the painting she had been promised. She wanted to make it a gift to her parents.

"We might as well get all the pictures out of storage," Buffy said. "The cops aren't interested in Leo anymore."

So Mercy again rented a van and with Dawn's help transported all Leo's artwork back to his studio. Dawn selected a medium-size portrait of herself to give her parents for Christmas. She also took possession of Leo's writings, including the little hand-made journal she had always loved so much.

# XXV
## BOOTSY

In the charmingly quaint community of Coyoacán in Mexico's Federal District, Leo happened one day upon a tiny *librería* in the process of going out of business. New books were marked down to half price and below; rare first editions were being offered for next to nothing. Leo knew almost immediately that this was his opportunity to provide himself a secure income, for he had now all but given up hope of ever being able to return to his old life. His first impulse was to buy up all the valuable old volumes in hopes of reselling them at a huge profit. Then it occurred to him that the bookstore itself would be a wiser investment.

Looking very like a penniless beggar, he asked the person in charge the price for everything. Although dubious that Leo could possibly be a serious buyer, the man quoted an amount not beyond Leo's means. Terms of the lease were satisfactory as well, and there were modest living quarters above. Leo flashed his bank roll, and an agreement was quickly reached.

The shop's owner of more than half a century had died recently, and his only heir, a dentist by profession, knew nothing about the business of bookselling. He wished only to liquidate his newly acquired assets as swiftly as possible. For Leo this appeared to be a fantastic stroke of good fortune. Of course, he would have to alter his appearance again. As a shopkeeper he should be somewhat presentable, but with a full beard and mustache, shoulder-length hair, and horn-rimmed glasses, Leo was hopeful that he would remain unrecognizable. Naturally, he would maintain the pretense of not understanding English.

The name above the shop door, *Lorenzo de la Paz*, was not the name of the owner immediately previous to Leo, but of the original owner in the nineteenth century. Leo adopted that name for his own. On the day the shop became his, he contacted a news agency and arranged to have several foreign newspapers, including the *London Times*, placed in his shop for sale to the public.

Customers were few; business was slow. But then overhead was extremely low, and Leo's living expenses were now greatly reduced. It quickly became evident that with frugality, Leo could survive here.

He yearned to resume his art career. There was so much in this immediate neighborhood that begged to be painted. And yet he dared not. If he were to remain at large, he knew that he must never do anything to draw attention to himself. Returning to the occupation for which he had been known in Texas—a high-profile occupation at that—was probably the single most-dangerous thing he could do.

And then on the Saturday before Christmas, the unthinkable occurred. Someone he had known before walked into his store. Robyn's roommate Bootsy, whom he had painted and then bedded in Austin the very weekend of Peggy's disappearance, entered with another American girl. To each other they spoke English, but Leo they addressed in Spanish. They were looking for a particular volume of poetry ten years out of print. Leo located a slightly worn copy signed by the author. They were extremely gratified and quibbled not at the extravagant price he set.

When they were gone, he breathed a sigh of relief. His disguise had proven adequate. But how, he wondered, had Bootsy not recognized his voice? He had often been told that his voice was quite distinctive. Did he sound different speaking Spanish than he did speaking English? Should he worry that his true identity might later dawn on Bootsy? Did she even know that he was on the lam? Would she keep her mouth shut, or would she mention having seen him in Mexico City?

There was nothing else to be done at this point. He had used up all his financial resources. He would simply have to brazen it out here and hope for the best.    The life of a fugitive is an uncertain existence at best and fraught with anxiety.

On Christmas Day he left the shop closed and went on a walking tour of Coyoacán and the adjacent neighborhood of San Ángel, where he happened to glimpse Bootsy again, this time from a safe distance. She and another woman (not her companion from the bookstore) were just getting out of a taxi, their arms full of gaily wrapped presents.    The house they entered was nothing less than a mansion.    Leo noted the address and returned home to a lunch of cold tamales and warmed-over beans.

Some of the foreign newspapers in Leo's shop went unsold every week, but there was always a demand for the *London Times*.    Leo was now selling two or three copies a week.    Of course, he still searched for Carmen's secret message, even though he no longer expected to find it.    And then one day, there it was.    He could barely believe his eyes.    He read the ad over and over.    It was genuine, no doubt about it.

Leo immediately closed his shop and hurried to the nearest post office to place a long-distance telephone call to Carmen.

"Oh, Papa, I'm so glad to hear from you.    I've been running that ad for weeks in the wrong paper. When you told me the *Times*, I just naturally thought of the *New York Times*, because we get that paper at home every week.    I completely forgot that your newspaper in London used to be the *Times*.    I couldn't understand why you didn't call.    Then finally last week it occurred to me what the problem must be."

Leo learned all he could from Carmen, then called Mercy to get the expanded version.    On Mercy's advice, he telephoned Detective Branson and

181

explained that he was in Mexico on business and had only today learned that the police had been interested in speaking with him. Was there still any question that he could answer? Branson said that personally he had lots of questions, but officially the case was closed.

As eager as Leo was in some ways to return to New Braunfels, he was equally reluctant to leave his new home here. In the first place, he felt that he absolutely had to continue operating this business in which he had invested the last of his life's savings. But no less important to him than that consideration was his desire to try to capture on canvas the look and feel of Coyoacán and San Ángel, and indeed, of Mexico itself.

He already missed Carmen and Brenda terribly, not to mention Dawn and the other little girls; and he missed his two good friends Mercy and Damien; but quite possibly, he missed Buffy most of all. In the few short months that she had lived with him, he had become fonder of her than he would have imagined possible.

Before leaving the post office, he decided to call her too. She was overjoyed to hear his voice. She had sold only one of his paintings, but she had got five thousand dollars for it. That would keep the household running until spring, at which time she meant to start taking pictures to art fairs and swap meets, especially the big one at Canton. Alba would be old enough by then to make the long trip in a car seat, and Mercy had expressed an interest in going along as well. In the meantime, if she ran short of money, Mercy would let her slide on the rent. So Leo was not to worry about her at all. She was doing well and looking out for his interests in New Braunfels.

The important thing, she insisted, was for him to get busy painting again.

Intending to do just that, he stopped at an art-supply store on the way home and purchased canvasses, paints, brushes, a collapsible easel, a palette and palette knife, fast-drying medium, linseed oil (which he used only rarely), and turpentine. Tomorrow, he would paint during the siesta hours, but today he needed to get the shop open again.

After closing that evening, Leo shaved for the first time in almost three months. Then with a pair of scissors, he trimmed his own hair. He would visit a barber shop as soon as he could conveniently do so. But for now, at least, the face in his mirror resembled the face he had used to see in his mirror before all the trouble.

As Fate would have it, Leo's first customer the next morning was Bootsy, and this time she recognized him immediately. Through Robyn, she had heard something of his difficulties. "But I thought that was cleared up ages ago."

"It was. It's just that until yesterday, I hadn't heard."

"How awful for you! And to believe I didn't even know you when I came in the other day!"

As Bootsy prepared to exit the shop with her purchase, a novel by Gabriel Garcia-Marquez, she invited Leo to call on her at her sister's house that afternoon. She would be returning soon to Austin and would very much like to introduce him to her family first. He would find them invaluable contacts, she promised.

And so when Leo closed for siesta that day, it was not to begin a painting after all, but to pay a visit on an old friend. The address Bootsy had given him was the same address at which he had seen her and another woman (her mother, he would later learn) arrive with Christmas presents only a few days earlier. Bootsy met him at the front door herself and showed him through the house to a stone-paved courtyard, around which the house seemed to curl itself. Large-leaf plants in thirty-gallon pots stood all about, creating a tropical oasis. At the center of that oasis was a swimming pool, in which two naked children splashed and cavorted whilst their mother, Bootsy's older sister Miranda, herself immodestly clad in only the bottom half of the briefest of string bikinis, watched over them from a wicker chaise shaded by an enormous beach umbrella.

Miranda was the same young woman Leo had seen in his bookstore with Bootsy. As he approached in Booty's wake, Miranda nonchalantly slipped into a crocheted cover-up, which, in fact, covered very little. Bootsy introduced Leo as an artist friend of hers from Texas. Quite obviously, Miranda did not recognize him from their previous encounter. When eventually Bootsy informed her that Leo had sold them a book of verse only a few days earlier, Miranda found it difficult to believe that this was the same gentleman.

A maid servant brought out lemonade and finger sandwiches. The two naiads, five-year-old Morgan and eight-year-old Madeleine, came out of the water long enough to eat and drink and be introduced to Leo. They had the same dark almond-shaped eyes and high cheek bones their mother and auntie had. When Leo expressed an interest in painting the little girls, their mother invited him to come back on Sunday afternoon and bring his art supplies.

"I'll be gone by then," Bootsy told him, "but Mother should be here. You really have to meet her. She works at the *Daily News*, and she knows everyone in the English-speaking community here."

"She knows a lot about bookselling too," Miranda added. "She used to work at the Librería Británica."

"Miranda and I grew up watching her pose for painters and fine-art photographers," Bootsy said. "She was always so beautiful and so elegant that both of us wanted to be just like her."

Bootsy flew back to Texas on Friday. On Sunday Leo painted a double portrait of Madeleine and Morgan that so pleased their father Geoffrey, an engineering executive at British Petroleum, he bought the picture on the spot and invited Leo to stay for dinner. Miranda and Bootsy's mother, Judith, did not, in fact, put in an appearance that day, but Miranda arranged for Leo to meet her the following week. Judith promptly embraced Leo as a dear friend and began introducing him to all the interesting people she knew, including expatriate writers, university professors, well-healed retirees, remittance men, diplomats, and a few corporate big wigs. She even helped Leo line up a lucrative rebinding job.

Every business-day afternoon during the siesta hours, Leo painted urban landscapes in those neighborhoods within easy walking distance of his shop. Sundays he devoted to figure painting. He had no difficulty finding models. He worked on smaller canvasses these days than those he had preferred in Texas. Consequently, he was able to complete pictures in much less time and offer them at lower prices. Soon his shop was as much an art gallery as a bookstore. On Judith's advice, he began stocking more and more books published in English. His business grew steadily, if not rapidly, and before long he was able to start sending Buffy money with some regularity.

In the spring, he offered Judith a full partnership in the bookstore on condition that she assume the management of it. She agreed without hesitation. Nowadays, if Leo worked in the store at all, it was just to relieve Judith whilst she ran errands. Unless he had book repairs or rebinding to do, he spent his days painting. As soon as he felt confident that Judith could handle the store by herself, he returned to Texas.

Carmen and Brenda picked him up at the airport in San Antonio, and he spent a few days with them before traveling on by bus. From the tacky little terminal in New Braunfels, he called Buffy to come pick him up. It was a happy reunion that followed. And when Dawn stopped by the apartment that afternoon, she squealed with surprised delight to find Leo there working on a painting of Buffy nursing Alba at the breast. This was just like old times.

After hugs and kisses, Dawn, still wiping tears of joy from her eyes, asked Leo, "Are you going to live here now? Or do you have to go back?"

"I plan to live here. This is my home, and I couldn't bear to stay away forever. Of course, I'll have to return to Mexico occasionally—maybe three or four time a year—but I should only be gone a couple of weeks each time."

"I have a surprise for you," Dawn told him, "I've been keeping it for you."

It was with great pleasure then that Leo accepted a copy of the first book to bear Dawn's imprint, a reproduction of his own personal journal, *Observations and Contemplations*, appropriately renamed *Observations and Contemplations of a Humanist*.

A week later, as a welcome-home gesture for Leo, Mercy held an ice-cream social in her backyard, inviting Buffy and Alba, Carmen and her family, Peggy and Starr, the Longs, the Ramseys, Damien Wynter, and the Flores-Hopewell clan. Each family that owned an ice-cream churn was to bring a different flavor of home-made ice cream. Damien asked for and received permission to come with a guest. His date for the evening turned out to be Jane Logan.

Leo, of course, took the precaution of putting out of sight those canvasses that the Ramseys might deem indecent. This precaution was not intended to deceive them, for Dawn had earlier informed him that her parents were now aware that he sometimes painted nudes. He simply meant to avoid the risk of offending their delicate sensibilities unnecessarily.

Brent and Helen had come to know Jennifer, Dulce, and Verity quite well, but they had never before met any of the parents of the three. This was also their first meeting with Leo. They were more than a little surprised to discover how likable all these radical liberals were. This evening was not an uncomfortable experience at all. Indeed, Jane's presence was an unexpected pleasure. As for Damien, he had been known to them only as a former teacher, whom their daughter admired and respected. Unaware of his long-ago difficulties with Reverend Wainwright, they had not formed a prejudice against him. They were thankful now for the opportunity to get to know him at last.

Toward the end of the evening, Leo managed to have a private word with Jane, whom he had only met for the first time tonight. He asked her whether she would consider posing nude for him. She smiled shyly and said that she would think about it and let him know in a couple of days.

www.ingramcontent.com/pod-product-compliance
Lightning Source LLC
Chambersburg PA
CBHW031111260626
47172CB00001B/317